The Mystery of the Masked Rider

Nancy woke with a start and sat up straight. For a second she was confused, but then the dim light from the stable aisle reminded her of where she was—in her sleeping bag in the stall next to Nightingale, her friend's horse.

Suddenly a rustling noise and the quick *clip-clop* of horse's hooves startled Nancy. Unzipping the sleeping bag, Nancy slipped out of it and put on her sneakers. Then she jumped from the cot and ran to the doorway.

A figure dressed in a black hat and cape was running down the aisle. Nancy blinked. I must be dreaming, she thought.

Then Nancy glanced in the opposite direction. Nightingale's stall door was wide open. In two strides Nancy was standing in the doorway. The stall was empty. Nightingale was gone!

Nancy Drew
Mystery Stories

Available from MINSTREL Books

NANCY DREW MYSTERY STORIES®

109

NANCY DREW®

THE MYSTERY OF THE MASKED RIDER

CAROLYN KEENE

A MINSTREL® BOOK

PUBLISHED BY POCKET BOOKS

New York   London   Toronto   Sydney   Tokyo   Singapore

A MINSTREL PAPERBACK *ORIGINAL*

 A Minstrel Book published by
POCKET BOOKS, a division of Simon & Schuster Inc.
1230 Avenue of the Americas, New York, NY 10020

Copyright © 1992 by Simon & Schuster Inc.
Produced by Mega-Books of New York, Inc.

ISBN: 0-671-73055-X

First Minstrel Books printing October 1992

10 9 8 7 6 5 4 3 2 1

NANCY DREW, NANCY DREW MYSTERY STORIES,
A MINSTREL BOOK and colophon are registered trademarks
of Simon & Schuster Inc.

Cover art by Aleta Jenks

Printed in the U.S.A.

Contents

1

Great Expectations

"Wow! Nightingale's turned into a gorgeous horse!" Nancy Drew exclaimed. She and her best friend, Bess Marvin, were standing in the center aisle of the barn at Fox Hollow Farm. An attractive young woman, her blond hair pulled back in a short ponytail, was leading a chestnut mare toward them. The horse's reddish-brown coat gleamed, and her muscles rippled.

"And what a sweetie pie," brown-eyed Colleen Healey said, ruffling the mare's mane. The blond girl, who lived with her parents on the small horse farm, had been friendly with Bess and Nancy in high school.

"I really lucked out when I bought her as a yearling," Colleen added. She halted the horse in front of Nancy and Bess. Ears pricked forward, Nightingale stared curiously at the two girls.

Then she nuzzled Bess's hand with velvet-soft lips.

"No wonder we haven't seen you in a while," Nancy said as she stroked Nightingale's white blaze. Nancy was casually dressed in jeans and sneakers. The eighteen-year-old's strawberry-blond hair fell below her shoulders. "Training your horse and going to all those shows must really keep you busy."

"Too busy," Colleen agreed with a sigh. Then she smiled. "At least that's what Phil would say."

Colleen had been dating Phil Ackerman ever since the girls had graduated from high school. Phil was a junior in college, so Nancy and Bess didn't know him well.

"Phil and I haven't had much time together lately," Colleen went on. "Actually, I haven't had much time for *anything* but riding, so I'm glad you two were able to come by this morning. It'll be fun having lunch together again. Plus, I want you to get to know Phil better. Because . . ." She hesitated and looked down at the toes of her paddock boots.

Nancy gave her a curious glance. "Is something wrong between you guys?"

"Oh, no, nothing like that," Colleen said quickly. "It's just that I've got some big decisions to make, and I guess I need advice from old friends."

"That's us," Bess said brightly. She wore

2

checked stirrup pants and a bright red top. Her black flats were already covered with dust from the tanbark particles in the aisle.

Colleen handed Nancy Nightingale's leather lead line, then bent down and picked up a brush from a tack box by the open stall door. "Seems as though things weren't nearly as complicated back in high school," she said.

"Want to talk about it?" Nancy asked.

Colleen nodded. Just then, the sound of tires crunching on gravel made the girls turn their heads toward the barn door.

"I wonder who that is," Colleen murmured as she walked down the aisle. "This place has been like Grand Central Station. Gloria Donner, a local trainer, showed up here at the crack of dawn." Colleen looked outside and groaned. "It's the San Marcoses. I told them not to come."

Puzzled, Bess looked at Colleen. "Who are the San Marcoses?"

"Oh, they own a big horse farm in Florida," Colleen explained. "Diego San Marcos and his daughter, Marisa, are in Illinois for the Midwest International Horse Show, which starts Sunday."

"That's tomorrow. Aren't you showing there, too?" Nancy asked as she led Nightingale up the aisle and stood next to Colleen.

"Yeah, but not until the last three days," Colleen replied. "Marisa's showing all week. They came a day early to let their horses get settled from the long drive."

The San Marcoses' silver Mercedes halted under a big oak tree.

"Looks like they're rich," Bess said from behind Nancy.

"Boy, are they," Colleen said under her breath. "And they'd do anything to get their hands on Nightingale." She reached out and grabbed the mare's halter protectively.

"Ah, Colleen!" a large man with thick black hair called as he climbed from the car. "There you are, señorita. And there's the beautiful Nightingale."

"Hi, Colleen!" A pretty girl of about fifteen bounced from the other side of the car. She had her father's thick black hair, but not his Spanish accent.

"Nightingale!" she squealed when she saw the horse. Running up, she took the mare's head between her hands and planted a big kiss on the horse's nose.

"Hi, Marisa, Mr. San Marcos," Colleen said in a formal voice. "I'd like you to meet two of my friends, Nancy Drew and Bess Marvin."

Diego took Bess's hand in his and, raising it to his lips, kissed the back. "Enchanted."

"Likewise." Bess blushed.

Before he could do the same to Nancy, she took his hand and gave it a firm shake. "Nice to meet you, Mr. San Marcos."

"I just couldn't wait to see Nightingale,"

Marisa told Colleen. "So I made Daddy drive me all the way up here."

"But it was my pleasure," Diego said. Taking the lead line from Nancy's hand, he led Nightingale into the sunlight.

Nancy glanced over at Colleen, who smiled as if to say it was okay. It seemed Mr. San Marcos was used to having his own way.

"Whoa, my beauty," Diego crooned to the mare. Nightingale halted. Arching her neck, she gazed curiously around her. Her white socks looked as though they'd been painted on her legs, and her copper-colored coat gleamed like a new penny.

"She is more perfect than I remember," Diego commented. "You have done a good job getting her ready for the show. Though if she were *my* horse—"

"But she isn't," Colleen interrupted. Smiling politely, she stepped forward and took the lead line from his hand. For a second Mr. San Marcos looked surprised. Then he bowed his head in a small nod.

"Not yet, anyway!" Marisa exclaimed. "Have you made up your mind, Colleen?" she asked eagerly.

"No, not yet, Marisa." Colleen shook her head. "I told you I'd make my decision after the show."

Marisa's face fell. "Is there anything we can do to change your mind?" she asked hopefully. "I'd love to take Nightingale back with us right now."

"No," Colleen said firmly. Nancy wondered if Marisa was going to make a scene. The young girl acted as if she was used to getting her way, too. But Marisa's face immediately brightened.

"I understand," she said. "It would be a hard decision for me to make, too. Can we see you school her?"

Colleen checked her watch, then looked over at Nancy and Bess. "Is that all right with you guys? We still have plenty of time before we meet Phil at the restaurant."

"Fine with me," Nancy said. "I'd love to see you ride."

"Me, too," Bess said. "As long as we're not late for lunch. I'm getting hungry."

Colleen laughed. "Still the same old Bess. Nancy, maybe you can help me tack up."

Fifteen minutes later Colleen was trotting Nightingale in a large ring behind the barn. Nancy, Bess, and the San Marcoses leaned on the top rail of the ring to watch the duo.

"Oh, Daddy, look at Nightingale move," Marisa said with undisguised admiration. "She practically floats. And her stride! I can't wait till she's mine."

Nancy looked sideways at the young girl. Marisa sounded awfully sure she was going to own Nightingale. Not that Nancy could blame her for wanting the mare. Even her untrained eye could tell that the horse was exceptional.

Quickly she glanced over at Diego San Marcos,

who was standing beside his daughter. His brows were drawn together in a serious expression. Abruptly he turned and smiled politely at Nancy, but there was a cold, calculating gleam in his dark eyes.

"Are you a rider, Miss Drew?" he asked.

Nancy shook her head. "Just for fun."

"I want to see Nightingale jump!" Marisa called.

Colleen nodded and turned Nightingale toward a crossbar. As the pair smoothly jumped it, Nancy thought horse and rider made a great team.

"Bravo!" Marisa clapped her hands, then turned to Nancy and Bess. "You should have seen Nightingale at the Columbia Classic Grand Prix. She was spectacular. It was her first grand prix, and she placed third."

"Wow," Bess said, impressed. Then she frowned in confusion. "So what's a grand prix?"

Marisa shot her a look of amazement. "Why, it's just the ultimate jumping class!"

"*Grand prix* means 'great prize' in French," Diego explained without taking his eyes off Nightingale. Colleen was heading the mare to an "in and out"—two fences so close to each other that the horse had only a stride in between them.

"The grand prix involves the highest fences," Diego continued. "Usually they're about four to six feet tall."

Bess whistled. "Wow. I'd be scared to death."

"Colleen's been really smart with Nightingale," Marisa chimed in. "She's taken it slow with the mare's training. Last month was Nightingale's first grand prix, but her performance showed everyone she's going to be the horse to watch at the Midwest International."

Colleen rode over to the fence and dismounted. "Show's over," she said with a grin.

"Come, Marisa," Diego said. "We're stopping at Gloria Donner's barn to see a young horse she has for sale." He nodded toward the girls. "Nice meeting you, Miss Drew and Miss Marvin. And Miss Healey, we will see you at the show. You and"—he paused a second, his gaze resting on Nightingale—"your lovely horse."

"Yes," Colleen said politely, but Nancy could tell she was uncomfortable. "And good luck, Marisa."

"You, too," the young girl said.

In silence the three friends watched as Diego and Marisa walked past the barn to the drive. Father's and daughter's heads were close together, as if they were in earnest conversation.

Colleen let out a sigh of relief. "Whew. I'm glad that's over with." She loosened Nightingale's girth and led her toward the gate.

"They sure seemed interested in buying Nightingale," Bess commented as they all walked back to the barn.

Nancy nodded. "That's for sure. Marisa acts as if she already owns her."

8

"I know." Colleen halted Nightingale inside the barn and began to pull off her saddle. "And Diego's so polite, but I don't know. I get these strange vibes from him."

"It seems as if he's used to getting what he wants," Nancy said.

"And what he wants is Nightingale," Colleen said grimly. She checked her watch. "I'll tell you the whole story on the way to lunch. We have an hour before we meet Phil. I've got to cool off Nightingale. She already has hay, so it'll just take a minute."

After Colleen finished her chores, the girls walked to the small ranch house. Nancy and Bess had sodas while Colleen took a quick shower and changed clothes. When she emerged from her bedroom, she was wearing a bright green jumpsuit and flats. Her blond hair was hanging free on her shoulders.

"Ready to go?" Colleen asked. "I've just got to turn Nightingale out into the pasture."

"I'll come with you," Nancy volunteered.

Bess offered to pull her Camaro around while the two girls went to the barn. Colleen turned into the small tack room for a lead line. Nancy went to Nightingale's stall and leaned over the half-door.

"Hey, girl," she greeted the mare. Nightingale was standing in the middle of the stall. Her head was down, and she was breathing so hard her sides were sucked in.

9

Nancy frowned. Something wasn't right. As Nancy turned to call for Colleen, Nightingale suddenly staggered sideways and fell to her knees. Then, with a loud groan, the mare rolled onto her side.

2

Poison Words

"Colleen! Come quick!" Nancy hollered as she threw the latch on the stall door. "Something's wrong with Nightingale!"

Lead line in hand, Colleen dashed from the tack room. Pushing past Nancy, she went into the stall and kneeled next to the mare's head. Abruptly Nightingale rose up on her front legs, then struggled onto all four. She twirled restlessly in a circle.

Colleen jumped back into the aisle just in time. "Looks like colic," she said breathlessly. "I've got to try and keep her calm. Will you call the vet, Dr. Hall? Her number's over the phone in the house."

Nancy nodded and ran from the barn. Bess was waiting in her car. When she saw Nancy rush past, she rolled down the window. "What's

11

wrong?" she called, but Nancy had no time to explain.

Ten minutes later Nancy had contacted the vet and was back in the barn, standing next to Bess. Colleen was leading Nightingale up the aisle toward them. The mare's neck was soaked with sweat, and she stumbled when she drew closer to the girls.

"I told the vet's office it was an emergency," Nancy told Colleen. "The receptionist said the vet would be here as soon as possible."

Colleen nodded, but her face looked white and drawn.

"I thought colic was just a stomachache that babies get," Bess said, frowning.

"Yes, but it's more serious in horses," Colleen explained. "When a horse's stomach gets upset, the pressure builds inside and can cause the intestines to twist."

Bess wrinkled her nose. "That sounds painful."

Colleen nodded. "So painful the horse can go into shock. That's why I'm trying to keep Nightingale moving. If she thrashes around in her stall, it might increase the risk of injury."

"Anything we can do?" Nancy asked, worried.

Colleen shook her head as she headed back down the aisle. "Just keep an eye out for the vet."

Fifteen long minutes later a dusty pickup rattled up the drive. Colleen led Nightingale into her stall to wait for the veterinarian. Dr. Hall, a tiny woman about forty years old, bustled inside.

"Let's take a look at you, Nightingale," the vet said as she dug into her medical bag. Nancy and Bess watched from the open stall door.

"Breathing's accelerated." Dr. Hall put a stethoscope in her ears and listened to the mare's heart. "So's the heartbeat." She placed the end of the stethoscope on the horse's flank, the area where the back leg met the body. "Lots of gurgling and rumbling in the intestines. Looks like your diagnosis was right, Colleen."

Bending down, Dr. Hall rummaged around in her bag and pulled out a big syringe. "First we'll give her a pain reliever and tranquilizer to calm her down."

The doctor plunged the needle into Nightingale's neck. Bess sucked in her breath, but the mare didn't seem to feel the shot. Nancy looked up at Colleen. Her friend's eyes were misty.

Dr. Hall gave Colleen's shoulder a pat. "Hang in there. We'll pump some mineral oil in her, and your baby will be as good as new."

Colleen sniffed and wiped her tears on her shirtsleeve. "I wish I knew what happened. She was cool when I put her in the stall. She had some hay left from this morning, but that's all."

"Could've been anything," Dr. Hall said. "Maybe something she ate."

As the shot took effect, Nancy could see that

13

Nightingale was beginning to relax. The mare's breathing slowed, and her eyelids drooped.

"Let's see if that helps," Dr. Hall said to Colleen. "I'll stick around for a while. Before I leave, though, I want to check out your feed. Maybe we can find out what did this to Nightingale."

Colleen patted Nightingale reassuringly, then unsnapped the lead line. Reaching down, she grabbed an armful of hay and carried it out of the stall. Nightingale gave a big sigh, then hung her head as if she were sleeping.

Colleen spread the hay on the floor of the aisle. While Dr. Hall put away her supplies, Nancy kneeled down and searched through the hay.

"Look at this," she said, holding up a green weed with three-inch-long leaves. "This isn't dry like the rest of hay."

"Let's show it to Dr. Hall," Colleen suggested. The three girls walked outside to the doctor's pickup.

"That's your culprit," Dr. Hall said after they'd handed it to her. "Bouncing bet."

"Bouncing bet?" Bess repeated. "That sounds like a dessert."

Dr. Hall laughed. "It would be the last dessert you'd want to eat for a while," she said. "Bouncing bet is a very poisonous weed. It won't kill you, but it gives you a pretty bad stomachache. Unfortunately, it grows wild around here." She shook

14

her head as though puzzled. "Though why it's in Nightingale's hay, I couldn't say. If it had been cut in the field and baled with the rest of the hay, it should be dry."

Nancy nodded in agreement. "It almost looks as if someone cut it fresh. Look. The bottom of the stalk was severed with something sharp, like a knife."

"That's crazy!" Colleen exclaimed. "Why would anyone want to poison Nightingale? It must've gotten in there by mistake," she added quickly.

"Then you'd better check all your bales of hay before Nightingale eats some more," Dr. Hall said firmly.

Nancy glanced at Colleen. Her friend was staring at the ground, but her cheeks were flushed. Did Colleen know something she wasn't telling them?

Dr. Hall checked Nightingale one last time. "She seems to be resting comfortably. The tranquilizer lasts for about an hour. If she's at all restless or in pain when she comes out of it, call me—pronto. I'll stop by this afternoon."

After the doctor had left, Nancy turned to Colleen. "I'll help you look through the other bales."

"Me, too," Bess offered.

Colleen sighed. "You and Dr. Hall are probably right, Nancy. Someone must have put the weed in Nightingale's hay."

15

"But who would deliberately want to hurt your horse?" Bess asked.

"The San Marcoses were here long enough to throw something in the stall," Nancy said. "And you mentioned that some trainer visited earlier. What did you say her name was?"

"Gloria Donner." Shaking her head, Colleen slowly began to walk down the aisle. "I can't believe the San Marcoses or Gloria would be involved. I mean, they have no *reason*. If someone wanted Nightingale, why would they put her in danger? I'd say it was just an accident, except . . ." She hesitated.

"Except what?" Nancy prodded gently. "Did something else happen to Nightingale?"

Colleen nodded. "Last week, when I went into the barn one morning, she was wandering loose in the aisle."

"Couldn't she have gotten out of her stall by mistake?" Bess asked.

"No," Colleen said firmly. "Right now, Nightingale's worth over one hundred fifty thousand dollars. If she does well in the Midwest International, her price will jump to two hundred thousand."

Bess sucked in her breath. "You're kidding!"

Colleen shook her head, her expression dead serious. "And when you own a horse worth that kind of money, you *don't* make mistakes like forgetting to lock the stall."

16

"Then how did Nightingale get out?" Nancy asked.

Colleen shook her head. "I have no idea. My dad and I don't keep the outside doors padlocked, in case a fire breaks out. But one or both of us is always home."

Nancy thought for a moment. "Then it sounds as though someone sneaked in at night."

Colleen nodded. "That's what my parents and I think. The row of white pines along the drive could have muffled a car motor. Since the night we found Nightingale loose, we've installed an alarm system. It buzzes in the house if anyone comes up the drive."

"Do you think someone tried to *steal* Nightingale?" Bess asked, her eyes wide.

"We don't know," Colleen replied. "My dad remembers hearing a noise that night and turning on the outside light. That may have been enough to scare off whoever it was."

"Wow." Nancy folded her arms across her chest. "This is developing into quite a mystery."

Bess shook her head. "They seem to follow you around, Nancy Drew."

"Any idea who—?" Nancy started to ask, but the roar of a car motor and the grate of tires on gravel stopped her in mid-sentence.

A car door slammed loudly. "Colleen!" an angry male voice hollered from outside the barn.

Colleen clapped her hand over her mouth.

"Oh, no! It's Phil! I forgot to call him about missing lunch."

"Well, surely if you explain about—" Bess began.

"What is going on!" Phil Ackerman stood in the doorway of the barn. His fists were propped on his hips. Nancy thought he looked like a gunfighter about to shoot. "I waited for over an hour for you!" Phil thundered.

"Oh, Phil, I'm so sorry." Colleen ran toward him. Nancy and Bess stayed back by Nightingale's stall. "You've got every right to be angry," Colleen said quickly. "We were on our way, but Nightingale got sick, and the vet just left. I completely forgot to call you."

Phil Ackerman's face went from pink to red. He glanced at Nancy and Bess, then grabbed Colleen by the elbow and pulled her outside.

"You could have called," he said, his voice a low growl. Nancy tried not to listen, but it was hard not to overhear.

Colleen murmured something, and then Phil's voice rose to an angry shout. "That's all you think about, isn't it? Well, this is the last time that stupid horse comes between us, Colleen. If you're going to be my girlfriend, you've got to give up Nightingale—or else!"

3

A Nasty Trick

Nancy watched in shocked silence as Phil Ackerman stormed across the gravel drive. Moments later his sports car zoomed down the drive in a cloud of dust. She couldn't see Colleen.

"Wow," Bess whispered. "What do you think that was all about?"

"I don't know, but he sounded plenty angry," Nancy whispered back. "Angrier than someone who'd just been stood up for lunch."

Bess nodded. "Maybe we'd better see if Colleen's okay."

Nancy and Bess walked to the outside door and peeked around it. Colleen was leaning against the barn wall, wiping tears from her eyes. With a halfhearted smile, she waved to them.

"So much for first impressions," she said with a sniff, taking the tissue Bess had hurried to hand her. "You guys must think Phil's a real jerk."

"We're not going to think anything until we hear what's going on," Nancy said.

"Thanks." Colleen blew her nose, then breathed deeply. "There, I feel better." She flashed a big smile, but Nancy could tell it was forced.

"How about some lunch?" Colleen asked, changing the subject. "If you don't mind tuna fish and carrot sticks, Healeys' Kitchen has great food."

"Sounds good to me." Bess linked her arm through Colleen's. "I'm so hungry, I could eat a horse!" Realizing what she'd said, she clapped her hand over her mouth in embarrassment. "Oops."

Nancy and Colleen burst into laughter as the three of them went into the barn to check on Nightingale. But when they passed the pile of hay in the middle of the aisle, Colleen's laughter died. "What a morning," she said under her breath.

Ten minutes later the girls were in the Healeys' kitchen, making tuna sandwiches.

"I'm sure glad Nightingale's better," Nancy said. "That was quite a scare."

"Boy, was it." Colleen poured out three glasses of juice and placed them around the table. "From now on I'm going to watch Nightingale like a hawk. Especially since . . ." Her voice trailed off.

"Since you don't think it was an accident?" Nancy asked as the girls sat down to eat.

Colleen nodded. "Something weird is definitely going on, but I have no idea what or why or who's behind it."

Bess glanced at Nancy, then back at Colleen. "Maybe telling us what's up between you and Phil might help," she suggested gently.

Colleen smiled. "Phil has nothing to do with Nightingale getting sick, believe me. He loves horses. That's how we met. We used to compete against each other in shows when we were younger. Then he quit riding."

"Why did Phil quit?" Nancy asked.

"Oh, he started playing soccer, and that took up most of his time. I'd practically forgotten about Phil until I bumped into him at the mall last year. Since then we've been going out—or *trying* to, anyway." Colleen frowned. "I spend so much time riding, preparing for shows, traveling, and helping my parents keep the farm up that our dates are pretty few and far between. It's no wonder Phil gets angry."

"I take it he's not interested in horses anymore," Nancy commented, reaching for a carrot stick. "Otherwise, maybe he could pitch in."

"He does help," Colleen said. "But you really have to give all of yourself if you want to get to the top in show jumping. Even my parents aren't as involved anymore. Your life becomes consumed by horses. Phil doesn't want that."

Nancy nodded. Now she understood why Colleen was thinking about selling Nightingale.

21

"And you're not sure you want that kind of life anymore, either?"

"You guessed it." Colleen pushed her plate away. Bess hungrily eyed her leftover half of a sandwich. Colleen laughed. "Take it, Marvin. I've suddenly lost my appetite."

"Thanks." Bess reached for the sandwich. "So the problem is, you don't want to sell Nightingale, but you don't want to spend so much time riding, either."

Colleen nodded, then stood up and went over to a cookie jar on the counter. "Right."

"Why don't you just keep your horse and ride for fun?" Bess asked.

"Because Nightingale's too talented to waste as a pleasure horse," Colleen replied. "I also have this dream of going to medical school. But that takes big bucks and major commitment."

"I'll say." Bess rolled her eyes. "Couldn't your parents help out?"

"Most of their money's tied up in the farm." Colleen set the cookie jar on the table and took off the lid.

Bess peered into the jar. "Mmm, chocolate chip. My favorite."

"And selling Nightingale would finance school," Nancy guessed. "Though you could postpone med school for a year or two."

Colleen sat heavily in the chair. "It seems as if I've waited long enough. My showing schedule is so crazy, I don't even have time to take classes. And the prize money isn't enough to cover Nightingale's expenses. She's actually costing me money. Besides, I love Phil, and I'd like to go to college with him. Campus life sounds fun."

"But you love Nightingale, too," Bess said with a sad smile.

"Yeah." Colleen looked gloomily down at the cookie in her hand.

For a few moments the three girls munched on cookies in silence. Nancy couldn't help but wonder if Colleen's information was tied in somehow with the poisoned hay. Could it have been Phil's way of discouraging Colleen from going to the show? Nancy sat back in her chair, her brow furrowed.

"Uh, oh," Bess groaned. "I recognize that expression, Detective Drew."

"Well, it is strange," Nancy said. "Why *would* anyone want to hurt Nightingale?"

"Maybe no one does want to hurt her," Colleen said. "I've been under such pressure lately, I could just be imagining things," she added, running her fingers through her hair.

Nancy went over and gave her friend a quick hug. "I don't think the bouncing bet was in anyone's imagination."

"Not mine, anyway," Bess joked. "I tend to imagine things like winning a million dollars."

The three girls laughed, and for a moment the

tension was broken. Colleen began picking up dishes and rinsing them off. Nancy cleared her plate and glass and handed them to her friend.

"You know, Colleen, I'd like to help if . . ."

"Gee, Nancy I sure would appreciate it if . . ." both girls started to say at the same time.

Bess brought over her dishes and handed them to Colleen. "I guess you two are trying to say the same thing," she explained. "And yes, it's a good idea for Nancy to take on the case."

"Though I've never had a horse as a client before," Nancy said with a grin. She turned to Colleen. "But seriously, if there is something strange going on, I'll try and track it down."

Colleen sighed. "That really would take a load off my shoulders. Maybe you can come out Monday to the barn and snoop around. Nightingale should be okay by then." She stuck the last plate in the dishwasher. "Right now I'd better check on my patient. Dr. Hall will be back soon."

"We should be going, too," Nancy said.

Five minutes later the girls said their goodbyes at the driveway. Nancy watched Colleen go into the barn, then slid into the passenger seat of Bess's red Camaro.

"She sure does spend a lot of time with that horse," Bess commented as they drove down the long, winding drive. "I can see why Phil gets mad."

"Though it did seem as if he went a little overboard," Nancy said with a thoughtful frown.

"I mean, I have to wonder what he meant by 'you've got to give up Nightingale *or else.*'"

"That's easy. He meant, 'or else we're breaking up.'"

Nancy folded her arms and rested her head back against the car seat. "Maybe."

Bess shot her a curious look. "You're not thinking Phil had something to do with Nightingale getting sick, are you?"

"It might make his life easier if the horse was out of the picture."

"No way." Bess shook her head emphatically. "I can't picture a guy being jealous enough to do in a horse."

"You're probably right." Nancy sighed. "I'm just glad we promised to come back Monday and do a little more investigating."

On Monday morning Bess and Nancy stood outside Nightingale's stall as Colleen finished putting on the mare's bridle. Nightingale's ears were pricked in eager anticipation.

"Boy, Nightingale sure looks different than when we left her on Saturday," Bess said.

"Dr. Hall said she's fully recovered," Colleen told her. "She checked Nightingale out yesterday afternoon." Colleen took the saddle off the door and threw it on the mare's back.

"And I'd say by the grin on your face that you and Phil made up," Nancy said in a teasing voice.

Colleen flushed. "You're right. Last night we

went out to dinner. It was very romantic. I guess I needed the break. I just didn't realize how much pressure I've been under lately, getting ready for the upcoming show and trying to make a decision about selling Nightingale."

"Has anything else unusual happened since Saturday?" Nancy asked.

"No. Things have been real quiet. Last night Dad stayed home and kept an eye on Nightingale." Colleen crossed her fingers. "Let's hope things have returned to normal. Right, girl?" She kissed Nightingale on her soft nose, then led her from the stall. But as the mare stepped into the aisle, Nancy could see that she was favoring her right front leg.

"She's lame," Nancy said, frowning. "Her front leg."

"What?" Colleen walked the horse two more steps down the aisle. Nightingale was clearly limping.

"I can't believe it!" Colleen's voice rose to a shrill pitch. "What is going on?"

"Maybe it's nothing," Bess tried to reassure her friend. "A pebble or something."

Colleen sucked in her breath. "You're probably right. I'm just overreacting. Oh, no!" Handing the reins to Nancy, she suddenly bent down and ran her hand down Nightingale's right foreleg.

"Look at this!" Colleen cried, straightening abruptly. She was staring down at the palm of her hand. Nancy came over to stand next to her.

There was reddish-brown gunk and horse hair on Colleen's fingers.

"What's that?" Bess asked, peering around Colleen's other side.

Colleen held out her hand. "Smell."

"No way!" Bess stepped back, but Nancy leaned over and sniffed. "It smells like strong pine tar," she said, wrinkling her nose.

"It's called a blister," Colleen answered in a bitter voice. "You rub the substance on a horse, and it burns its skin sore. My fingers are tingling right now."

Puzzled, Nancy frowned. "If you didn't put it on Nightingale, then who did?"

Colleen's eyes glimmered angrily. "I don't know. But whoever did it was trying to make Nightingale lame on purpose!"

4

A Painful Surprise

"Someone deliberately rubbed the blister on Nightingale's leg?" Nancy repeated, shocked.

Colleen nodded. "And it must have been late last night or sometime this morning. Nightingale was fine when I put her in the barn early yesterday evening."

"But why would someone want to hurt your horse? And where'd they get that blister stuff?" Bess asked two of the questions that were spinning in Nancy's mind.

Colleen threw up her hands. "Who knows!" she exclaimed. "If I knew who it was I'd . . . I'd . . ." Suddenly her voice trailed off and her shoulders slumped. "I'd better get some warm soapy water and wash off the blister before it makes Nightingale's leg swell," she said finally. "It's already burning my own fingers." She held out her hands. Her fingers were reddish brown. "The stuff stains your skin, even if you wash it off."

By the time Colleen returned with a bucket, Nancy and Bess had untacked Nightingale and put on the mare's halter. "I figured you wouldn't be riding today," Nancy said to Colleen.

"That's for sure," Colleen said grimly. "I just hope Nightingale's going to be in shape for the show. It's only four days away." Bending down, Colleen began sloshing the sudsy water onto the mare's legs. "Fortunately, one application of a blister doesn't really hurt a horse. And whoever put it on didn't use much. It probably made Nightingale's skin tender, so she didn't want to bend her pastern."

"Uh, I don't want to sound too dumb," Bess said hesitantly. "But what's a pastern?"

Colleen pointed to what looked like the horse's ankle. "It's between the hoof and the fetlock." Colleen stood up, and Nancy caught a whiff of the strong scent of the blister.

"The blister will wear off overnight," Colleen said with a sigh. "But this makes three days in a row I haven't worked Nightingale. And she needs to be in super shape if she's going to do well at the show."

"What exactly is a blister and where could someone get it?" Nancy asked.

"A blister is a counterirritant that you rub on a

horse's leg. It's supposed to make sprains and pulled tendons heal faster."

"Huh?" Bess looked confused. "How can making a horse's leg sore help it heal?"

"When the blister burns the area, it supposedly speeds up the flow of blood to the leg, which promotes healing. It's used a lot on racehorses. Most people who show horses don't use it, because it can peel off the hair."

"Do you keep a bottle in your tack room?" Nancy asked.

Colleen nodded. "In the medicine chest. I haven't used it in ages."

Nancy handed Bess the lead line. Inside the tack room she found the medicine chest mounted on the wall. Opening the door, she read the various labels. Finally she found the blister tucked behind a box of cotton. When she pulled out the bottle, she checked for signs that it had recently been opened. But there was no telltale scent of the strong-smelling liquid, and the top was screwed on tightly.

"Whoever put the blister on Nightingale didn't get it from your medicine chest," Nancy said when she rejoined her friends, who were standing outside in the driveway. Colleen was hosing off Nightingale's legs.

"That doesn't mean anything. You can buy blister at any tack shop," Colleen said.

"Still, only someone familiar with horses would know about it."

Colleen snorted. "That's just about everyone I know."

"Could someone you're competing against in the International have done this?" Nancy asked.

"Maybe," Colleen replied with a shrug. "But they'd be taking a big risk for nothing. I mean, the blister won't keep me from showing."

"True." Nancy fell silent as Colleen wiped down her horse's legs. Who could have sneaked in and put the blister on Nightingale? It had to have been someone who knew about the Healeys' alarm system.

"Colleen, what time did you and Phil come in last night?" Nancy asked.

Colleen stood up. "About midnight, I think."

"And was the driveway alarm on?"

"Yes. My dad said it woke him up when we came home."

"Hmmm." Nancy began to pace the gravel drive. "So the person who did this had to know how to avoid the alarm system." Abruptly she halted in front of Colleen. "Did you hear Phil's car leave after he brought you home?"

"Sure. He came in for coffee and then . . ." Suddenly Colleen's eyes narrowed, and she gave Nancy a suspicious look. "Are you trying to pin this thing on Phil?"

"No. But he *is* a suspect. Everyone is," Nancy added quickly. She knew how mad people got when someone close to them was accused of wrongdoing.

"Well, forget it," Colleen said firmly. "Phil might be jealous of the time I spend with Nightingale, but he'd never do anything to hurt her. He knows how much she means to me."

"Okay." Nancy decided to back off, even though Phil was her most likely suspect. He knew about the alarm, he knew his way around the barn, and he had been at the Healeys' farm. He even had a motive. Maybe Bess thought jealousy wasn't a strong enough reason for Phil to try and hurt Nightingale, but Nancy wasn't so sure. One thing was certain: There was no use pressing the matter if Colleen was being adamant about Phil's innocence.

"Okay, so let's look at the people who were here the morning Nightingale got sick," Nancy began. "Why don't you tell me more about Gloria Donner, that trainer you mentioned?"

"Let me turn Nightingale out in the paddock first," Colleen said, taking the lead line from Bess. "A little grass will take her mind off her leg, and we can watch her from the porch. Besides," she added, wiping the perspiration off her forehead, "I could use a soda."

Colleen led Nightingale to a lush pasture, where a fat Shetland pony was grazing. When he saw Nightingale, he raised his head and whinnied. Opening the gate, Colleen turned the mare loose, then draped the lead line over the fence.

Nightingale trotted two faltering steps, then

stopped to sniff noses with the pony. He squealed and pawed the air. Then the two ducked their heads and began to graze side by side.

"That's Jester, my old pony," Colleen told Nancy and Bess as they walked toward the house. "I learned to ride on him. Now he's just company for Nightingale."

Fifteen minutes later the girls were lying comfortably on deck chairs with sodas in hand. It was a perfect October day—cool and crisp, yet the sun felt warm on Nancy's skin. Colleen's parents were both at work.

"Okay, now back to Gloria Donner," Colleen began as she relaxed back in her lounge chair. "She's a trainer who has a small stable about half an hour from here. Nightingale and I have taken a few lessons from her this year. If I continue to show grand prix, though, I'm going to need a full-time trainer. I was thinking about hiring Gloria, and she seems pretty eager to take us on."

"Well, that rules her out," Bess said, reaching for a bowl of chips. "She'd have nothing to gain if Nightingale got sick. If I were you, Nancy, I'd concentrate on the San Marcoses. Diego seemed kind of ruthless to me. Charming, but ruthless."

"Mmmm." Nancy slowly sipped her soda. "Except what would *they* gain if Nightingale was hurt?"

Colleen shook her head. "Marisa has been competing against me all year. We both showed in the amateur-owner jumper classes. I usually beat her, but I can't see them resorting to something this low to win. Besides, at the International, Marisa's going to be riding amateur-owner while I'm riding grand prix."

"What does amateur-owner mean?" Nancy asked.

"Amateur means you're riding for pleasure, not for money like a professional. An amateur still gets the prize money if she wins, but someone can't hire an amateur to ride a horse. I decided to start riding grand prix because there's more money in it, and if Nightingale's successful in that level of competition, she'll be worth more, too."

"Got it," Nancy said. "And now that you and Marisa are riding in different classes, there's no reason for the San Marcoses to sabotage your horse."

"Right," Colleen agreed. "And since they want to buy Nightingale, they certainly wouldn't want to see her hurt. Besides, you saw Marisa. She's crazy about Nightingale."

Bess gave a rueful chuckle. "The mystery gets curiouser and curiouser. I think, Colleen, that there's only one thing for you to do."

"What's that?" Nancy and Colleen asked in unison.

"Hire two horse bodyguards to go with you to the International Horse Show."

For a second Colleen looked confused. Then

she burst out laughing. "Oh, I get it—you mean I should take you and Nancy!"

"Right!" Bess cried. "The only thing we'd be missing out on this weekend is a Halloween party Nancy and I were invited to."

"I don't have a costume, anyway," Nancy added. "And I'd rather see the show."

Colleen's face broke into a big smile for the first time since they'd discovered that Nightingale was lame. "Wow. I can't think of anything I'd like more. It'll be fun."

Seeing Colleen so happy, Nancy had to smile, too.

Just then an earsplitting *br-r-ring, br-r-ring* pierced the air. Bess jumped a foot off the lounge chair, spilling her chips. "What was that?"

Colleen laughed. "The driveway alarm. I left it on this morning. Someone must be coming. Maybe my mom's home from work early." Standing up, she squinted through the row of white pines. A green sports car was zipping up the drive. "It looks like Phil," she said happily.

Nancy and Bess started to get up, too, but Colleen gestured for them to stay seated. "You guys relax. I'll bring him over."

She ran to meet Phil. Nancy could see his tall figure getting out of the car. Colleen met him in the drive and gave him a big hug.

"I'd say they made up," Bess said under her breath.

"Looks that way," Nancy said, her tone grim.

Bess gave her a curious glance. "You still think he's guilty, don't you?"

Nancy shook her head. "I don't know for sure, but—"

Colleen's cheerful voice cut off her sentence. "Nancy, Bess, I'd like you to meet Phil Ackerman, the love of my life."

"The second love of her life," Phil interjected with a playful grin. "I think Colleen's first love is Nightingale."

"No way." Colleen punched him gently on the arm.

Nancy stood up. She could see why Colleen was crazy about Phil Ackerman. He was tall and dark, with a slim yet muscular build and a dazzling smile.

"It's nice to meet two of Colleen's oldest friends," Phil said, reaching out to shake Bess's hand. Then he turned to Nancy. "You must be Nancy Drew, the famous teen detective."

"I don't know about the *famous* part," Nancy said with a smile. Taking his hand, she shook it firmly. When she did, she glanced down. On the top of his wrist was a reddish-brown stain.

A shiver ran up Nancy's spine. The spot on Phil's arm was the same color as the stain on Colleen's fingers after she'd touched the blister. That meant one thing—Phil Ackerman must have put the blister on Nightingale's leg!

5

Sharp Moves

Nancy couldn't believe it. The stain seemed to be proof that Phil was the one who'd sneaked into the barn last night and applied the blister. Colleen had said the reddish-brown color lingered even after it was washed off.

Phil turned back to Colleen and threw his arm around her shoulders. "How's Nightingale today?"

Colleen rolled her eyes. "You wouldn't believe what happened," she said. Pulling him down next to her on the lounge chair, she began telling him about the morning.

Nancy looked up at Phil Ackerman. His dark brows were drawn together in what seemed to be genuine concern.

Maybe I'm jumping to conclusions, Nancy thought. Maybe he got a trace of the blister on him from hugging Colleen.

"At least there wasn't any permanent damage to Nightingale," Bess said when Colleen had finished.

"Thank goodness." Colleen let out a sigh of relief, but her smile had turned into a small frown. "But that doesn't mean something else won't happen to her."

Phil took Colleen's hand. "Well, I have some news that will cheer you up," he announced. "I'm taking off two days of school and going with you to the show. I might have to study a couple of nights, but otherwise, I'm all yours."

"Really?" Colleen's face broke into a huge grin, and she threw her arms around him. "That's terrific!"

Yeah, terrific, Nancy thought. Unless Phil was the one behind Nightingale's injuries. She couldn't get the idea out of her mind.

"Nancy and Bess are going, too," Colleen told Phil. "They're going to help watch over Nightingale."

"That's great," Phil said. Nancy watched closely to see how Phil took the news, but he just smiled and turned back to Colleen.

"Then it's settled." Colleen sat back with a satisfied expression on her face. "Thursday morning we'll all meet here at the barn—seven on the dot."

"Seven in the *morning*?" Bess squeaked. "But Nightingale probably won't be awake."

"Oh, she'll be awake," Colleen assured Bess. "And you will be, too, Bess Marvin!"

"Even the sun's smarter than us," Bess said sleepily on Thursday morning. She was hunched down in the passenger seat of Nancy's Mustang, her eyes shut. "It's not up yet."

Nancy chuckled. She herself had gotten up at five-thirty to pack a small suitcase and roll up her sleeping bag for the three-night stay at the show. Then she'd picked Bess up at six-thirty sharp to make sure they'd get to the Healeys' barn on time.

"Just remember, it was you who volunteered us for groom duty," she said.

"Ummmph. But I said bodyguard duty," Bess pointed out. "That sounded easy. I figured we'd just sit around the show and watch Nightingale."

"Well, we'd look pretty obvious if we weren't doing something," Nancy said. "A groom is a perfect cover."

"But we want to look obvious," Bess protested. "That way no one will try anything."

"True. Only I want to *catch* whoever injured Nightingale. That's going to be trickier."

Bess stifled another yawn. "I'm just glad nothing's gone wrong since our visit Monday."

Nancy nodded in agreement. "Me, too. Let's keep our fingers crossed that nothing else happens."

39

Flipping on the turn signal, Nancy steered the Mustang up the Healeys' drive. When they reached the barn, they could see the soft gleam of lights coming from the half-open door. Phil's sports car was already parked next to a pickup that was hitched to a horse trailer.

When Nancy and Bess walked into the barn, they met Phil standing in the middle of the aisle, holding Nightingale. "Morning." He nodded his head.

"Good morning." Colleen greeted the girls with a cheery smile. She was kneeling in the tanbark, wrapping bandages around Nightingale's front legs.

Bess gasped. "Nightingale didn't get hurt again?"

Colleen laughed. "No. These are leg wraps. They protect her legs when she rides in the trailer."

Bess let out a relieved sigh.

Colleen stood up. "Are you guys ready to help load up the truck?" She pointed to a pile of boxes, bales of hay, and blankets.

Nancy nodded, then pulled a reluctant Bess toward the pile. "Come on, sleepyhead. A little exercise will wake you up."

An hour later Nightingale and all her equipment had been loaded onto the truck and trailer. After saying goodbye to her parents, Colleen secured the trailer doors and checked the hitch.

Then she climbed in the driver's seat. Nancy sat in the middle, and Bess was by the window. Already, Bess had her jacket scrunched into a pillow and was settling down for a nap.

Nancy chuckled. "She needs her beauty sleep."

Colleen laughed, too, as she started the pickup and headed down the drive. Phil was following in his car.

"If nothing happens, we should be there right after lunch," Colleen said. "I packed some sandwiches so we can eat in the car. That way we'll get there in time for me to work Nightingale in the ring before my first class tomorrow."

"What class are you riding in?" Nancy asked.

"Friday night is the Gambler's Choice Jumping Stakes. That's really a wild class. The riders can take their horses over the fences in any direction or order they want."

"Wow," Nancy said. "How do you decide which way to go?"

"Each fence is assigned a number of points from ten to one hundred and twenty. You only have eighty seconds, so you try and jump the fences worth the most points."

"And if you knock down a fence, you don't get the points," Nancy guessed.

Colleen nodded as the truck rumbled up the ramp onto the highway. "You can't ride a course that's too tricky, or your horse will have trouble.

41

But to win you have to make some sharp turns and really pour on the speed."

"It should be exciting to watch." Nancy checked in the side mirror. Phil's car was still right behind them. "And what about Saturday night?"

"That's the night of the big Worthington Cup Grand Prix. The horse and rider who win first place get five thousand dollars in prize money," Colleen told Nancy.

Nancy whistled. "That would almost pay for a year of med school. If you and Nightingale keep winning, you won't have to sell her."

"I wish." Colleen sighed. "Unfortunately, the expense of showing eats up most of the profits. And if I do keep competing, I'll have to hire a trainer like Gloria Donner, and she'll want a percentage of my winnings."

Nancy shook her head. "Then how do people afford to keep showing?"

"Some of the riders turn professional," Colleen explained. "That means they get paid to ride and train other people's horses. Some pros are good enough to get a sponsor—that's a company willing to pay expenses in return for publicity."

"And some people, like the San Marcoses, just have lots of money," Nancy added.

"Right," Colleen answered.

Nancy tried to digest all of the information. The sport of show jumping was a lot more complicated than she'd thought. It wasn't going to be easy to track down the person who'd injured Nightingale.

From what Colleen had told Nancy, there was no reason for either the San Marcoses or Gloria Donner to try and hurt Nightingale. That left Phil, or some unknown person. At least Phil would be easy to keep an eye on.

As they rode along the highway, Colleen told Nancy and Bess about the layout of the stable area and show arena, and where they'd be staying. Nancy listened intently, knowing that every bit of information would be important.

Several hours later Colleen pulled the truck and trailer into a vast parking lot by the Capital Center arena. The lot was filled with trucks, trailers, and large vans. Two huge tents had been erected over temporary stalls.

Colleen parked in front of an aisle leading into the stable area. A closed gate barred the aisle's entrance. Outside the tent, people were washing, leading, and grooming horses. Under the tent Nancy could see several mounted riders walking their horses.

"O-o-o-o," Bess groaned when she jumped from the truck. "I'm stiff from sitting so long."

Colleen laughed. "Just think how poor Nightingale feels. She's been standing in one position, swaying back and forth, for four hours." She went around to the back of the trailer and swung

43

open the top door. A whinny of greeting came from inside.

"Let me help you unload her," Phil said as he came toward them. He'd parked in an empty space several rows away. Opening the side door in the trailer, he ducked inside and unsnapped Nightingale. Nancy and Colleen lowered the back ramp.

"Ready?" Colleen called up to Phil.

"Ready."

Colleen unlatched the padded bar behind Nightingale's rump. Cautiously the mare backed out as Phil held on to the lead rope.

"Nightingale! You're here!" A squeal made Nancy turn. Marisa San Marcos was hurrying through the gate. She was dressed in a black, pin-striped hunt coat, which was tailored to cut in at the waist and flare at the hips. She also wore white riding breeches, tall, shiny black boots, and a black velvet hunt cap. Marisa's sharp-looking outfit was completed by a white silk choker, secured by a sapphire-studded pin.

"How's it going, Marisa?" Colleen asked as she took the lead line from Phil.

"Oh, okay." Marisa wrinkled her nose to show that she wasn't completely happy. "Topflight won a third, but he knocked down a jump in Tuesday's class. He's such a fabulous horse, but he just doesn't have that urge to win like Nightingale."

Beaming up at the mare, Marisa patted her on the neck. "Well, gotta go. I'm jumping again in

44

half an hour. What number is Nightingale's stall, so I can come visit her?"

"Twenty-nine," Colleen told her.

"Maybe I'll see you later, then." With a wave, Marisa headed back under the tent.

"Isn't Topflight the horse the San Marcoses paid a hundred thousand dollars for?" Phil asked.

"A hundred thousand dollars!" Bess gulped.

"Yeah," Colleen replied. "Topflight's a good jumper, too. But the San Marcoses don't want just good. They want the best."

"Where should we start taking this stuff?" Nancy asked. She'd raised the door on the cap covering the bed of the truck and was pointing inside.

"Stalls twenty-nine and thirty," Colleen called. "I'm going to walk Nightingale around a while to get the kinks out." She started to lead the mare to a grassy knoll at the far end of the parking lot.

"I'll take the tack trunk," Phil said, pushing past Nancy. He lowered the tailgate of the truck and pulled out a large chest. "Meet you there." Grabbing onto the two end handles, he lifted the trunk and headed down the aisle.

"Great," Bess grumbled. "We get to unload three bales of hay, a bag of grain, all Colleen's riding clothes, and four suitcases."

Nancy laughed. "Some of that stuff is going to our rooms at the motel. Come on, we can tackle a bale of the hay. Colleen will probably want some in the stall for Nightingale to munch on when she gets back."

Bess gave her a look that said, "You're crazy," but Nancy reached in, slipped her fingers under the baling string, and slid the hay bale onto the end of the tailgate.

"Ready?"

Bess sighed. "It's not in my bodyguard contract, but here goes."

Nancy and Bess swung the hay off the tailgate. Then, with one of them holding each end, they carried the bale into the stable area. The aisle was shaped like a T, and the girls stopped at the intersection at the center of the stable. "Which way now?" Bess said panting.

Nancy set down her end of the bale and checked the aisle to the right. "Not that way. These numbers are in the forties. Must be to the left. I don't see Phil, though. I wonder where he went?"

"Who cares," Bess grunted as she picked up her end again. "Let's just get this over with."

They walked down the left-hand aisle. About halfway the aisle again split into another T.

"Don't tell me," Bess groaned. "Another mile to go."

Nancy laughed. "No. I think it's the next right."

As they made the final turn, Nancy fleetingly saw someone stride from a stall and disappear around the next corner. In the dim light she couldn't tell if it was a man or woman. But when Nancy and Bess made their way down the aisle, Nancy realized that the person had come from stall twenty-nine—the stall assigned to Nightingale.

"I wonder who that was." Nancy set the bale outside the doorway and frowned. The stall door was open.

Bess slumped down on the bale. "Who?"

"The person who came out of this stall." Nancy peered inside. It had been freshly made up with clean straw.

"I didn't see anyone." Bess wiped her brow. "I was too busy sweating."

Nancy stepped into the stall. The straw looked undisturbed. Nancy swept her foot through it and heard the sound of metal clinking on the concrete floor.

Quickly, Nancy bent down and began sifting through the yellow stalks.

"What are you doing?" Bess called from her seat in the doorway.

"I'm looking for"—Nancy found something, and she held it up for Bess to see—"this." She added grimly, "A very sharp nail."

6

Intruder in Disguise

Bess jumped up from the hay bale. "A nail! Nightingale could have stepped on it."

Nancy nodded. "It wasn't pointing up, but still, it could've bruised her foot . . ."

"Or worse." Bess shook her head.

Nancy knelt in the straw. "Help me look, okay? I want to make sure there aren't any more nails."

Bess crouched down beside Nancy. Silently the two of them searched through the straw.

"What's going on?" Colleen said, peering in the doorway.

"Nancy found a nail," Bess explained. "Wait, here's another one."

"And look, two more." Nancy held them up for Colleen to see.

Colleen's mouth fell open. "Oh, no. I was hoping all this would be over once we got to the show."

"Afraid not." Nancy checked through the straw one last time, then stood up. "It's safe. Go ahead and lead Nightingale in."

"I just don't get it," Colleen said as she walked the mare into the stall. "Who could be doing all of this?"

"Nancy saw someone coming out of the stall," Bess said.

"I didn't get a good look at whoever it was," Nancy admitted. "He or she was moving at a pretty fast pace in the opposite direction." She pointed down the aisle. "And the person had a hunt cap pulled low over his or her face."

"Hey, what's that?" Bess asked. She headed in the direction Nancy had indicated and bent down to pick something up. It was a black face mask decorated with red sequins.

"That's weird." Nancy frowned as she took the mask from Bess.

Colleen shut the stall door and came up beside them. "Not that weird. Saturday is Halloween, remember? And there's going to be a costume class that night. It's kind of a tradition of this show, and everybody gets into it—a break from the tension, I guess."

"Why aren't you riding in it?" Nancy asked.

Colleen shrugged. "With all the things happening to Nightingale lately, I decided against it."

Holding the mask, Nancy walked slowly back to Nightingale's stall. "Whoever threw those nails in here could have dropped this by mistake." She hung the mask over the door latch. "Maybe someone will come to claim it."

"Claim what?" Phil's voice boomed behind her, and Nancy jumped. He was still carrying the tack trunk. With a smile he set it down in the aisle.

Nancy wondered what had taken him so long. Had he darted around the other way and thrown the nails into the stall?

"That trunk must have been awfully heavy," Nancy said in a lighthearted voice. "We beat you here by ten minutes."

"I stopped and talked to some old friends," Phil replied. Then he caught sight of the mask, and his face clouded over. "I thought you weren't riding in the costume class," he said to Colleen.

"I'm not. Bess found—"

"Well, *there* you are," a male voice interrupted Colleen. "It's about time."

Nancy turned to see a slim, attractive young man with dark brown hair striding up the aisle toward them. He was wearing riding boots, breeches, and a denim shirt, the sleeves rolled partway up. His smile was friendly as his bright green eyes darted from face to face, settling on Colleen.

"Hey, Scott." Colleen stepped forward to give him a hug. "I figured if I came late, it would give you a chance to win some prize money this week," she teased.

Scott laughed. "Isn't that the truth!"

"Nancy Drew and Bess Marvin, meet one of my rivals, Scott Weller."

"Nice to meet you." Bess instantly stuck out her hand and flashed her most winning smile.

"You came, too, huh, Ackerman?" Scott turned to Phil, who had a sour look on his face.

"Sure did, Weller. Someone had to keep an eye on you," Phil replied in a joking voice, but Nancy noticed a hint of jealousy in his expression. "We wouldn't want you winning everything."

"Oh, he won't." Colleen moved away from Scott to stand next to Phil. "So how's it going, Scott? Tough competition?"

Scott nodded. "Yeah. France and Canada have some great riders here." He walked over to peer into Nightingale's stall. "But I haven't seen anything so far that'll beat the wonder horse."

Colleen blushed, but Nancy could tell she was pleased by his comment. "Except maybe the Stanleys' horse, Wintergreen," Colleen said quickly. "Isn't that who you're riding?"

"Right. And Formidable, too."

"Scott's a professional rider," Colleen explained to Nancy and Bess. "He rides for several different owners."

"For now," Scott added, a trace of bitterness in his voice. Then his face brightened. "Are you guys going to the Halloween party tonight?"

"I didn't know there was a party," Colleen said.

51

"The Stanleys are hosting it," Scott said. "They have a suite at one of the hotels. It's going to be a blowout."

Bess clapped her hands. "Sounds like fun—" she began, but a jab from Nancy's elbow cut off her sentence.

"Since Bess and I will be busy grooming Nightingale, we won't be able to go," Nancy said. "But you should, Colleen."

"No, really, I'd better . . ." Colleen started to say, but Nancy gave her a firm look.

"You need to go," Nancy murmured. "I'll explain later."

"Sounds fun," Phil said. "Do we have to wear costumes?"

"Most people will," Scott said. "The party starts at nine." He turned toward Nancy and Bess. "Sorry you can't make it, but maybe I'll see you later."

"That would be nice." Bess grinned.

When Scott walked away, Bess said to Colleen, "Boy, he's cute."

Phil snorted. "He thinks he's some hotshot rider, too."

"That's because he is," Colleen said. "Scott would have made it to the Olympics last time if his horse hadn't been injured."

"I thought I heard a tiny bit of bitterness in his voice when you mentioned he was riding as a professional," Nancy said.

"It's a sad story." Colleen sighed. "Scott had a

wonderful horse, but she fell in a jumping class and broke her leg. It ended her career. She wasn't insured, and Scott couldn't afford to buy another horse, so he had to turn professional. He'd had his heart set on the Olympics, but they don't accept professional riders, so he was pretty upset. Fortunately, he's doing great now. All the owners want him to ride for them, so he gets his pick of the top horses."

"Listen, we'd better get the rest of the gear in," Phil said abruptly. He seemed to be tired of hearing about Scott. "And we need to pick up the exhibitor badges."

"Why don't you guys get the badges, and Bess and I will finish unloading and watch Nightingale?" Nancy suggested to Colleen.

"Good idea. Thanks." Colleen tossed Nancy the truck keys. "We'll stop by on our way back and park the truck." She waved, then walked hand in hand with Phil toward the arena entrance on the other end of the stable.

Bess slid the hay bale in front of Nightingale's stall, then sat down and leaned back against the door.

Nancy laughed. "I take it that means I'm unloading and you're guarding."

"You got it." With a grin, Bess pulled a granola bar out of her jacket pocket. Nancy declined her offer of a bite, then headed back out to the truck.

On the way she saw Diego San Marcos striding down the aisle. Curious, Nancy followed him.

Marisa had known what stall Nightingale was in. Had she told her father so he could plant the nails before Colleen led Nightingale in?

He would have had time, Nancy thought. But why would he want to? If Diego and Marisa were that interested in buying Nightingale, they certainly wouldn't want to injure her.

Then an idea struck Nancy. Maybe they weren't really interested in buying the mare. Maybe they were just pretending to be. That was a possibility, Nancy told herself with a sigh, but it still didn't explain what the San Marcoses' motive would be.

Diego turned and went into a stall. When Nancy got closer, she saw a series of three wooden signs hanging on each stall door. Each sign had a horse's name engraved on it in blue letters, then the words M & M Farms and The San Marcoses underneath. A big banner was strung at the top of one of the stalls. It said, Champion Jumper—Miami, Florida. Several ribbons hung off the banner. It was easy to see that Diego San Marcos and his daughter were into showing—big time.

As Nancy approached the last stall, she heard two people arguing. She could hear Diego's deep voice with its Spanish accent. The other voice sounded like Marisa's.

"I'm going, Father, whether you like it or not." Marisa's voice sounded shrill.

"No, you aren't," Diego said firmly. "You are

here to ride horses. I am doing everything possible to ensure that you will win. Now you must do your part. And no more arguing!" Then he spun from the stall, practically running into Nancy.

"Hello, Mr. San Marcos," Nancy said quickly, trying to cover up the fact that she had been eavesdropping. "Remember me? Nancy Drew, Colleen Healey's friend," she added when Diego looked momentarily confused.

"Ah, yes. The young lady who only rides for fun. And what are you doing at the show, Ms. Drew?"

"Oh, just helping Colleen. And learning more about show jumping. It's quite exciting."

"Hi, Nancy!" Marisa called from the stall. Nancy peered inside. The young girl was standing on an overturned bucket, braiding a horse's mane. The horse wore a blue and white blanket, and Marisa was weaving blue and white yarn into the horse's mane. "Sorry I can't stop. Mr. Sunshine here rubbed out some of his braids, and I need to get them in before his class."

"Mr. Sunshine?" Nancy queried. "I thought you said your horse's name was Topflight."

Diego laughed. "You have a lot to learn about the horse world, Ms. Drew. M and M Farms has many horses. Some are young and green like Mr. Sunshine, so Marisa rides him in Green Hunter classes. Maybe he'll be talented enough to go into jumper, and maybe we'll sell him." He shrugged. "Who knows?"

Marisa nodded in the direction of the other stall. "Topflight's over there, and next to him is Golden Glory. This is Mr. Sunshine's first year showing jumper, but I think we're going to try him in the Worthington Cup."

"You must be busy!" Nancy said, impressed.

"Totally." Marisa patted down a braid, then jumped off the bucket. "But I love it—especially the winning part."

"I must go, Ms. Drew," Diego said in his formal voice. "Some business matters to take care of." He smiled at Nancy, then gave Marisa a stern look. "I will see you at exactly four o'clock in the warm-up ring."

"Yes, sir," Marisa said politely. But when Diego left, she turned to Nancy and rolled her eyes. "Fathers!"

Nancy laughed. "I know what you mean."

"But if it wasn't for my father, I couldn't do this," Marisa said as she unbuckled Mr. Sunshine's blanket.

Nancy leaned against the doorframe. She was dying to find out what Marisa and Diego had been arguing about. And what had Diego meant when he said, "I am doing everything possible to ensure that you will win"?

"Are you going to the party tonight?" Nancy asked in a casual voice. Father and daughter might have been fighting about a night out.

"I wouldn't miss it." Marisa giggled. If Diego

had forbidden her to go, Marisa didn't seem the least bit worried about it.

"Is your father going, too?"

"No way," Marisa scoffed, but then she lowered her voice. "Fortunately, he has a meeting with some business partner or something." She slid the blanket off the horse and carried it into the aisle.

"Are you wearing a costume?" Nancy asked, thinking about the red and black mask.

Marisa's eyes sparkled mischievously. "Yeah, and it's wild. I'll show it to you."

She glanced up and down the aisle as if to make sure no one was looking, then kneeled down in front of a big trunk. After opening it, she rummaged beneath piles of horse bandages and brushes and pulled out a fancy dress wrapped in a plastic bag.

Nancy's eyes widened when she saw the costume. It was black with red sequins—exactly like the mask Bess had found outside Nightingale's stall!

7

Food for Thought

"What a beautiful costume!" Nancy exclaimed as Marisa pulled the plastic off the dress and held it up.

Trying to cover her surprise, Nancy pretended to admire the fancy dress. The red sequins swirled across the black bodice in a sunburst design. The short, full skirt was made of red chiffon.

"Does it have a mask?" Nancy asked, suppressing her excitement. "That sure would make it perfect."

"Yeah, it does." Bending over the trunk, Marisa hunted through the equipment. "But I don't see it. I hope it didn't fall out when I pulled out the horse blankets. I had to hide it in here so my dad wouldn't see it," she confided in a low voice.

Nancy's mind whirled with questions. If the

58

mask in the aisle was Marisa's, when had she dropped it? Was she the person who'd been in Nightingale's stall? Nancy wished she'd gotten a better look at the person. But with their identical hunt caps and breeches, all the riders looked alike.

Nancy watched as Marisa carefully folded the dress and hid it under some leg wraps. "I take it you don't want your dad to see the costume," she said.

Marisa giggled. "You know fathers. Not only doesn't he want me to go to the party, but he wouldn't like the grown-up dress, either." She sighed. "Sometimes he's just so old-fashioned . . ." Suddenly she stood up and gave Nancy an embarrassed smile, as if she'd realized she'd revealed too much. "Well, I'd better get back to work."

"Me, too. Maybe I'll catch you in your next class." Nancy waved, and Marisa disappeared into Mr. Sunshine's stall.

On the way to the truck Nancy thought about the San Marcoses. Diego was a strict taskmaster, but Marisa was also very ambitious. For them, showing was big business, with high stakes. And now Marisa had said she was riding in the Worthington Cup, which meant she'd be competing against Colleen after all. Now the San Marcoses had a very good reason for wanting Nightingale out of the picture. The red and black mask might be just the evidence Nancy needed to

59

prove that Diego or Marisa had thrown the nails into Nightingale's stall.

When she reached the truck, Nancy hurriedly unlocked the door of the truck cap and pulled out half a bag of grain. She didn't want to leave Bess alone with Nightingale any longer than necessary.

Half an hour later Phil and Colleen had relieved Nancy and Bess of their duties. Nancy had shared her information about the San Marcoses with Bess, but not with Colleen. She didn't want Phil to know what she'd discovered.

"I need to exercise Nightingale in the warm-up ring," Colleen said. "Why don't you two grab an early dinner? It may be your last chance."

"Are you sure you'll be okay?" Nancy asked.

Colleen gave her a reassuring smile. "Phil will be here, don't worry."

"That's what I'm worried about," Nancy muttered to herself as she and Bess headed down the aisle.

"What are you mumbling about?" Bess asked.

"I don't like leaving Colleen and Nightingale alone with Phil."

Bess stopped in her tracks. "Do you still think he's guilty?"

"Phil is one of my main suspects."

"After all you found out about the San Marcoses? I mean, even though they were in Florida the night Colleen found Nightingale loose in the barn, they could have hired someone to steal her."

"Don't worry. Diego and Marisa are high on my list, too." Nancy pointed to a wide door through which a stream of people and horses was moving in and out. "That must be the entrance to the arena."

"This place is huge," Bess said as they walked through the doorway and out into an open area, filled with riders exercising their horses. The floor had been covered with tanbark. Several jumps had been set up along one side. A walkway bordered the other side. The only thing separating pedestrians from horses was a rope strung between a row of wooden poles.

"This must be where Colleen's going to warm up Nightingale," Nancy said. "And look, there's the entrance into the show ring." She pointed to a high, solid gate that was just being opened to let out a horse and rider.

"Our next contestant is Elsa Van den Berg, aboard Stowaway," the loudspeaker system blared into the warm-up area and across the whole arena. Nancy watched as a rider in hunt clothes jogged a sleek gray horse into the ring.

"I wonder where the food is?" Bess mused as they headed down the walkway.

In front of them Nancy could see the entrance to a double stairway. "Over there, I bet," she said, leading the way.

At the top of the stairs the girls stepped into a crowded walkway the width of a city street. Concession stands and booths lined both sides. The booths were selling everything from artwork to horse feed.

"This is the concourse Colleen was telling me about," Nancy said. "It circles the arena."

Bess's eyes bugged out. "You mean there are booths around this entire arena?"

Nancy laughed. "Yup. A hundred and twenty of them."

"Oh!" Bess clasped her hands. "I've died and gone to heaven." Immediately she set off toward a display of silver jewelry. Nancy grabbed her arm.

"Let's get some food first. Then you can shop until you drop."

Bess nodded. "Good idea. I'll need the strength."

The girls found a small cafeteria-style restaurant. Nancy picked out juice, a salad, and a turkey sandwich. When she glanced at Bess, she saw that her friend's tray was heaped with food.

"Over here!" someone called as they were paying the cashier. Nancy looked across the crowded room. Scott Weller was gesturing from a corner.

She wound her way through the tables and set her tray opposite his. "Hi. You're not showing tonight?"

"Not until eight." He gave her a friendly smile.

"That's why I'm eating now. It'll give my food a chance to digest before I get prejumping jitters."

Nancy sat down and poured her juice. She noticed Scott had finished eating. "I'm surprised that someone who's been competing as long as you still gets nervous."

Scott shrugged. "I never totally relax. But that's good, I guess. It gives me that edge I need to win."

"Whooo. This weighs a ton." Setting her tray down, Bess slid into the seat next to Scott. He chuckled when he saw all her food.

"All I had for lunch was a skimpy sandwich," Bess quickly explained.

Nancy laughed. "And a granola bar and a . . ."

Her friend held úp her hand to silence her. "Colleen said we may not get a chance to eat later, remember?"

"Have you girls known Colleen long?" Scott asked.

"Since high school," Bess answered, biting into her hamburger. "How about you?"

"Oh, I started competing against Colleen and Nightingale about two years ago in amateur-owner jumper classes."

Nancy stopped chewing. "Colleen told us what happened to your horse. That must have been tough."

"It was, at the time. But I got over it. You can't be sentimental in this business."

"What happened to your horse?" Bess asked. "Colleen said she couldn't jump anymore."

"She slipped and fell on some wet footing at a show. She broke her leg in two places, so they had to put her down."

Bess looked confused.

"That means the vet had to put her to sleep," Scott explained in a matter-of-fact voice. "It's almost impossible to put a cast on a horse."

Bess flushed. "Oh, I'm really sorry."

Nancy put down her sandwich. No matter how casual Scott acted, she could tell by his downcast eyes that he was still upset about the death of his horse.

"So, let's talk about something different," he said finally. "What do you think of Nightingale?"

"She's terrific," Nancy said. "Not that either of us knows much about horses," she added.

"And we haven't really seen her jump anything very high," Bess said.

"Why's that?" Scott raised his brows.

Immediately Nancy shot Bess a warning look. She didn't want her telling anyone about Nightingale's injuries.

"Uh," Bess stammered. "Because this is the first time we've seen Colleen show her."

"Oh." Scott settled back in his chair, as if satisfied with her answer.

"Since you showed amateur-owner, did you also compete against Marisa San Marcos?" Nancy asked. Maybe Scott knew something that might help Nancy with the case.

Scott shook his head. "No, fortunately. Marisa and her father are like two barracuda. They'd do anything to win. Don't get me wrong. Marisa is a super rider for someone her age, and Diego buys the finest horses."

That's just what Nancy had thought.

"The year that Marisa started in amateur-owner, I went professional," Scott continued. "Colleen rode against her all year, though." He chuckled. "Much to Diego's dismay."

"Why's that?" Nancy asked.

"Because Colleen always beat Marisa, no matter which horse she rode. It really ticked off old Diego. He wants to be number one."

"I got that feeling, too," Bess said. "That's why he wants to buy Nightingale."

Scott's brows raised in surprise. "Colleen's going to sell Nightingale?"

"I think you'll have to ask Colleen about that," Nancy told him.

Bess flushed again. "Me and my big mouth. I figured everyone knew."

"Well, we'd better be going." Nancy stood up. "Maybe we'll get to watch Colleen exercise Nightingale."

"Not me!" Bess exclaimed. "I can hear those little booths calling to me, 'Bess, Bess, come spend some money.'"

Nancy and Scott laughed.

"I'll walk down with you," Scott told Nancy. The three of them dumped their trash, then headed out of the cafeteria. Bess waved goodbye and disappeared into the crowd walking around the concourse. Nancy and Scott went down the steps. At the bottom they had to show their exhibitor badges.

The warm-up area was full of horses in western-style tack.

"The next class must be cutting horse," Scott said. "That's where the horse is judged on how well it can separate a cow from the herd. It's pretty neat to watch."

A truck pulling a long trailer rumbled into the area. In the back of the trailer a dozen cows snuffled and bellowed.

Standing on tiptoe, Nancy looked around for Colleen. Her friend was trotting Nightingale in small circles on the other side of the warm-up ring.

"They make a great team, don't they?" Scott nodded in the direction Nancy was looking. "I don't understand why Colleen would ever want to sell Nightingale."

"Whatever her reasons, it can't be an easy decision." Nancy tried to sound vague. She glanced sideways at Scott as they started down the walkway toward horse and rider. "Isn't it unusual for you and Colleen to have stayed such good friends? After all, you're rivals, right?"

"Well, yes and no," Scott replied. "It's true that when big prize money's involved, horse people tend to get greedy. At the same time you spend half your life showing. You see other riders more than your family. If you didn't make friends, you'd be really lonely."

Just then Colleen caught sight of her friends and waved them over. Nancy waved back and started to duck under the rope.

"Watch out!" Colleen yelled suddenly.

Nancy looked up, and her heart flew into her throat. A riderless horse, reins hanging loose, was galloping straight for her!

8

Bumps in the Night

Nancy felt strong hands yank her backward. Losing her balance, she fell in the tanbark as Scott ducked under the rope and raised his arms.

"Whoa!" he yelled.

The galloping horse snorted and veered away from him. Colleen reined Nightingale into the horse's path. "Whoa," she echoed Scott's command.

The runaway horse slid to a stop, then lunged to the right. Wheeling Nightingale in a circle, Colleen boxed the horse into a corner. At the same time a rider in cowboy hat and chaps rushed up.

"Whoa, Minx," the rider crooned. With a snort Minx tossed his head, pranced a few steps, then finally halted.

"Are you all right?" Scott turned to Nancy after the rider had caught his horse.

"Fine." Nancy stood up and brushed off her jeans. "Thanks to you."

"I should have warned you to watch out," Scott said. "When this many horses are packed into a small space, you're bound to have trouble."

"Hey, are you two okay?" Colleen trotted over on Nightingale.

Nancy nodded. "That was some pretty good rounding up you did," she teased. "Maybe you two should be in the cutting class."

Colleen laughed. "I don't think we're quite ready to tackle cows yet."

"Hey, sorry about that." Minx's owner came up to them, his now-docile horse walking beside him. He gave Nancy a concerned look. "Are you all right?"

She nodded and smiled to show him she was fine.

"This is my horse's first show in an indoor arena," he explained. "The truck pulling the cows spooked him."

"Don't worry, we understand," Scott said. "It's happened to all of us at least once."

The cowboy tipped his hat and walked off.

"I'd better be going, too," Scott said. "The Stanleys will be nervous if I'm not ready for my class an hour early."

"Good luck," Nancy and Colleen both called to him.

"What's he competing in tonight?" Nancy asked Colleen when Scott had left.

"The National Open Jumper class," Colleen replied.

"Why aren't you entered in that?"

"Nightingale's still young, so I don't want to push her," Colleen told her. "Two jumping classes is enough for us to handle."

Colleen dismounted and pulled the reins over Nightingale's head. As they walked back to the stable area, Nancy told her friend about her conversation with Scott.

"Bess didn't mean to blurt out about your thinking of selling Nightingale," Nancy explained.

Colleen shrugged. "Well, everybody will have to know sometime. If I do decide to sell, the San Marcoses won't be the only ones who'll be interested."

"Speaking of the San Marcoses . . ." Nancy began. She told Colleen about Marisa's costume.

"You mean the mask in the aisle was Marisa's?" Colleen asked in a shocked voice.

"I'm not positive, but I think so," Nancy said. "Did you know that Marisa was riding in the Worthington Cup?"

Colleen shook her head. "No. It'll be her first grand prix event."

"It also gives her a reason to want Nightingale out of the class."

Colleen stopped walking and stared at Nancy in disbelief. "No way. Marisa's one of the most talented young riders on the East Coast. Not only wouldn't she jeopardize her career doing something stupid like sabotaging Nightingale, but she doesn't *need* to. She's good enough to win on her own."

"Maybe *she's* good enough, but what about her horses?"

"Okay, so they're not as good as Nightingale," Colleen conceded. "But she still wouldn't resort to sabotage. She loves Nightingale too much."

"Do you think all that cooing over your horse could be an act?"

"No!" Colleen said firmly. Clucking to Nightingale, she led the mare into the stable area.

Nancy caught up to them, and they walked down the aisle in silence. Colleen was having a hard time believing that anyone she knew could be a possible suspect, and Nancy understood that. Still, her job was to find out who was guilty, even if it did upset her friend.

"What about Diego?" Nancy asked finally. "Even Scott said that Diego would do anything to win."

"I don't know," Colleen said. She sounded angry. Then her shoulders slumped. "It's not that I don't want to help you, Nancy. But you're asking me to accuse people I've known for years. People who I've always thought were honest."

Nancy reached over and squeezed Colleen's arm. "I know it's hard," she said. "But—"

"So there you are," Phil called, walking toward them. He had a plastic dry-cleaner's bag draped

71

over one arm. "Are you ready to head back to the motel and dress for the party?" he asked Colleen.

"Oh, I don't know," Colleen said halfheartedly. "I really shouldn't leave Nightingale alone. I think I'll just set up the cot in the extra stall and turn in early."

"No way!" Nancy protested. "Bess and I will sleep here and keep our eyes on Nightingale."

"Well . . ." Colleen looked undecided.

"I want you to go," Nancy insisted. "That way you can keep an eye on your rivals." She gave Colleen a meaningful look. Then she turned and pulled the mask from its hiding place behind a bucket. "I also want you to present this to Marisa and see her reaction."

"Oh, all right," Colleen said finally. "But I'm not wearing a costume."

"Oh, yeah?" With a grin Phil held up the plastic bag by a hanger. "Check this out," he said, pulling up the plastic. Underneath was a gold-embroidered outfit with filmy harem pants—a costume straight out of the *Arabian Nights*.

Colleen drew in her breath as she touched the shimmering bodice. "Phil, it's beautiful. Where'd you get it?"

"Let's just say I rubbed my magic lamp, and out jumped a genie who gave it to me."

"Oh, right." Colleen laughed. Nancy was glad her friend had relaxed again. She was also glad that Colleen and Phil were going to the party. That would keep Phil out of the way.

"And what are you going to wear?" Nancy asked Phil as she started to unsaddle Nightingale.

He frowned. "Well, that's a problem. Any suggestions?"

Just then Bess came striding down the aisle toward them. She was carrying a cowboy hat. "Look what I bought!" she said, plopping it on her head.

Grinning, Nancy looked back at Phil. "Well, how about the Wild West look?"

"Let's see," Bess said, holding up her watch later that evening. Squinting, she tried to read the numbers in the dim light from the stable aisle. "It's eleven o'clock, which means that everyone at the party is feasting on crab-stuffed mushrooms and spiced shrimp." She sighed. "And here we sit in a cold, smelly stall listening to a horse chew its hay."

Nancy laughed at her friend. Bess was sitting on the edge of one of the cots they'd set up in the stall next to Nightingale's. Nancy was stretched out in a sleeping bag on the other cot, her jacket scrunched into a pillow. "At least we won't gain any weight from too much rich food," Nancy teased.

"Oh, I don't know about that." Leaning over, Bess rustled around in her backpack and pulled out two packages of cookies and a bag of chips. "Reinforcements."

Tossing a package to Nancy, Bess settled back on her own cot. Both girls began to quietly munch their cookies. Nancy heard the rustle of straw as Nightingale turned in her stall. All evening they'd kept a sharp eye on the mare. Now that the stable had quieted down and most of the people had left, Nancy thought it was safe to relax a little.

"At least Colleen's having fun," Bess said a moment later.

"And she's keeping an eye on Phil and Marisa," Nancy added. "If everyone's at the party, it'll make our job easier." She yawned and rubbed her eyes. "Whew, it's been a long day."

"I know what you mean." Bess kicked off her sneakers and slid into her sleeping bag. "This cot's not as bad as I thought."

"Mmmm." Nancy yawned again. "Actually, it's kind of comfortable," she mumbled. Pulling the sleeping bag up to her chin, she snuggled down under it. The hushed sounds of the stable were lulling. Nancy could see Nightingale's rusty coat through the slats of the stall wall. Glancing at Bess, she noticed her friend had already fallen asleep. Maybe I should stay awake and watch Nightingale, Nancy thought, but her eyes were heavy. Soon she was asleep, too.

Hours later Nancy woke with a start and sat up straight. For a second she was confused, but then the dim light from the stable aisle reminded her of where she was. Checking her watch, she noticed it was four A.M.

Suddenly a rustling noise and the quick *clip-clop* of horse's hooves startled Nancy. She decided she'd better check Nightingale.

Unzipping the sleeping bag, Nancy slipped out of it and put on her sneakers. Then she jumped from the cot and ran to the doorway. A figure dressed in a black hat and cape was running down the aisle. Nancy blinked. I must be dreaming, she thought.

Then Nancy glanced in the opposite direction. Nightingale's stall door was wide open. In two strides Nancy was standing in the doorway. The stall was empty. Nightingale was gone!

9

A Very Close Call

Nancy's mind raced as she grabbed a lead line and dashed down the aisle the way the costumed figure had gone. Frantically she hunted right and left for Nightingale. Had Colleen arrived early to exercise her? Or had the figure in black stolen the valuable mare?

At the intersection Nancy stopped, held her breath, and listened. The stable was quiet. Suddenly, a low nicker and answering whinny came from the left. Then Nancy heard the *clip-clop* of hooves once again. It had to be Nightingale.

Nancy took off down the aisle, screeching to a halt at the second T. With a gasp of relief she saw Nightingale ambling in the opposite direction. There was no sign of the costumed person. When the mare stopped to poke her head into a stall, Nancy approached her, hand extended, palm flat as if she had a treat.

76

"Whoa, girl," she crooned. "Whoa, Nightingale."

The mare turned her head and eyed Nancy curiously. Then Nancy looked beyond Nightingale and noticed the bluish glow of the parking lot lights. Someone had left the metal gate wide open.

Nancy's heart quickened. She had to catch Nightingale before the mare panicked and dashed for freedom!

"Look what I've got for you," Nancy said, still holding out her empty hand. Slowly she walked toward the mare. "It's really nothing, but if you let me catch you I promise we'll go back to your cozy stall, and I'll give you a bucket of grain. How does that sound?"

Nightingale pricked her ears. Nancy held her breath. Three more steps and she'd be able to grab the mare's halter.

Just when she was almost close enough to grasp the leather strap, a loud clang made Nancy jump. Nightingale threw her head up and wheeled around, then raced for the open gate.

"Whoa, Nightingale!" Nancy cried, but it was too late. The gate was only fifteen feet ahead, and the mare wasn't going to stop.

Suddenly a stocky figure leapt from a stall doorway and, holding up its arms, hollered, "Whoa!" Surprised, Nightingale slid to a halt. The split-second stop was all the person needed to reach up and grab the side of the mare's halter.

Nightingale reared and started to scramble backward, but the person held tight. Nancy ran up and quickly snapped on the lead line. When she turned, she could see that the person was a woman with close-cropped hair.

"Thanks," Nancy managed to gasp before Nightingale, still excited, snorted and pranced sideways. Reaching up, Nancy ran a soothing hand down the horse's sweaty neck. "Easy girl," she said. "You're all right."

"You and your horse doing a little sleepwalking?" the woman asked when Nightingale had finally calmed down.

"Uh, no," Nancy stammered. "I'm afraid she got out."

The woman raised one eyebrow. "Better be more careful next time," she said gruffly. Then, noticing Nancy's flush of embarrassment, she added, "Accidents happen to everyone. I should know."

Nancy wondered what the woman meant. "Well, thanks again. I don't know who left the gate open." Nancy nodded toward the end of the aisle. "Did you see anyone around?"

"Nope. I was back in the corner of the stall, braiding a horse's tail. Besides, people don't usually get here until six or later." The woman strode over and swung the gate shut. She had an athletic build and wore a down vest and paddock boots. Her face was deeply tanned, and squint lines fanned out from her eyes, as if she spent a lot of time outdoors.

"Whoever left that gate open ought to be more careful," the woman declared in a no-nonsense voice. "Your horse could have gotten onto the highway. It's a good thing I heard you holler. But I know I shut the gate an hour ago when I came in."

Nancy straightened in surprise. "You got here that early?"

The woman nodded. "Of course. When you've got five horses to groom and braid before they compete at eight in the morning, you don't get much sleep."

"You're going to ride five horses?"

She laughed. "No. The three spoiled girls I work with are riding them. Only they partied all night and won't bother getting up until the last minute."

The woman gave Nightingale a curious look, then glanced back at Nancy. "Isn't that Colleen Healey's mare?"

Nancy nodded. "Right. I'm helping Colleen. My name's Nancy Drew."

The woman stuck out a hand and shook Nancy's with a firm grip. "Gloria Donner."

"Gloria Donner?" Nancy's brows shot up. She remembered Colleen telling her about taking lessons from someone named Gloria Donner. "You're a trainer, right?"

"That's me. And boy, would I love to work more with Colleen and Nightingale." She patted the mare's neck with solid slaps. "This here's one talented animal."

"I know. But if I don't get her back in her stall, she'll be one talented, sleepy animal," Nancy said. "Nice meeting you, Gloria."

"Likewise. And you tell Colleen I'll be around to see her."

Nancy waved and started down the aisle with Nightingale. When she turned right, she saw an overturned metal bucket in the middle of the concrete floor. That was what must have made the clang, Nancy thought. Had someone deliberately dropped it to scare Nightingale?

Nancy turned the bucket over with her foot. It was an ordinary bucket with no clues as to whom it belonged to.

Instead of going back to the stall, Nancy led Nightingale up and down each aisle, looking for signs of the costumed person. There were several kids sacked out on cots and in sleeping bags, but no one she recognized. When she went past the San Marcoses' stalls, everything was dark and quiet.

That didn't mean anything, Nancy decided. Anyone could have sneaked in and out of the stable—Phil, Marisa, Diego. She'd have to ask Colleen if she remembered a black-caped costume at the party. It was just too bad Gloria hadn't seen the person who left the gate open.

With a sigh Nancy walked Nightingale back to her own stall. The mare walked in and immediately stuck her nose in her empty feed tub.

"All right, piggie." Nancy laughed. "I guess you deserve a treat."

"What's going on?"

Nancy turned and saw Bess standing in the doorway of the extra stall. Her friend's hair was tousled, and her eyes were heavy with sleep.

"Nightingale got out," Nancy explained as she tossed a handful of grain in the mare's bucket.

"Huh?" Bess looked bewildered.

As Nancy closed the stall door, she scrutinized the latch. "Looks okay to me. And I know I checked and double-checked it last night. That means someone opened her door and deliberately let her out."

Rubbing her eyes, Bess shook her head. "But there was nobody around."

"Not true." Nancy told her friend about the person wearing the cape and about Gloria Donner. "And somebody left the gate to the parking lot open, too."

"Wow. It's good Gloria was there, or Nightingale could have bolted for the parking lot."

Nancy paused in thought. "It was an amazing coincidence that Gloria was the only person near the open gate, and that she just happened to save Nightingale at the right time."

"I know you're figuring something out, but you've lost me," Bess said with a shrug.

"What if Gloria let Nightingale out, just to play the hero and save her?" Nancy mused. "Colleen might feel indebted to Gloria and definitely decide to hire her as her trainer. Gloria is obviously eager to work with Colleen and Nightingale."

"None of what you're saying makes sense," Bess grumbled. "Why would Gloria want to hurt Nightingale?"

"I don't know. It's confusing to me, too. Must be because it's only five A.M." Nancy stifled a yawn. "I guess we both should try and get another hour of sleep. This place will be busy pretty soon." Stepping past Bess, she went into the extra stall. "Give me a hand, will you?" She grabbed one end of her cot.

"What are you doing?" Bess asked.

"My job. I'm going to sleep in front of Nightingale's door."

Bess helped Nancy carry the cot into the aisle. Nancy shoved the bed up against the stall door and flopped down on it.

"Now let somebody try and get her," she announced. Ten minutes later the two girls were once again asleep.

"Nancy," a voice called softly.

"Hmmm?" Nancy opened her eyes. Colleen was sitting on the edge of the cot, an amused tilt to her mouth.

"Boy, you sure take your job seriously!" Col-

82

leen laughed. "I didn't mean you had to sleep *with* Nightingale."

"Oh." Nancy sat up and rubbed her eyes. Checking her watch, she saw that it was seven A.M. Up and down the aisle people and horses were moving in all directions.

Colleen held out a steaming carry-out cup of hot chocolate. "Drink up. You two must have had an exciting night to sleep through all this noise. I couldn't rouse Bess."

Nancy snapped the top off the cup and took several sips. "Mmm. Delicious. Thanks. And you're right. We *did* have an exciting night."

"What happened?" Colleen jumped up from the cot and peered into the stall. "Is Nightingale okay?"

"Yes. Somebody let her out, though." Nancy told her friend everything that had happened.

"Thank goodness for Gloria," Colleen said. Then she smacked her fist into her hand. "I knew I shouldn't have gone to that party."

"Hey, it turned out all right," Nancy reassured her. "Did you find out anything?"

Colleen shook her head. "I gave Marisa the mask and told her I'd found it in the aisle. She seemed genuinely puzzled, but who knows? That was some sophisticated outfit she had on," she added, her eyes twinkling. "Then I asked her why she was riding in the Worthington Cup. She just said it was about time she started grand prix level. Then she said, 'Especially if I'm going to be riding Nightingale.' " Colleen chuckled. "That kid's determined to own my horse."

"Was anyone wearing a Zorro costume?" Nancy continued. "I saw someone running down the aisle in a black hat and cape right before I noticed that Nightingale had disappeared."

Colleen thought for a minute. "I don't think so. But there were a lot of people there."

"What time did the party break up?"

"I don't know. It was still going strong when Phil and I left about midnight. He dropped me off at my room, then went to his."

"You saw him go in his room?"

"No, but I'm sure he did," Colleen said emphatically. With a sharp look at Nancy she spun on her heels and went into the extra stall. A minute later she came out with several sections of hay. "Bess is still zonked out."

Nancy pushed her cot out of the way. "Let me go in with you," she said. "I want to check out the stall. Maybe there's a clue that will tell us who let your horse out last night."

As soon as Nancy opened the stall door, Nightingale came over and snuffled her cheek in a friendly greeting.

"At least this time she wasn't hurt," Colleen said as she walked around the mare, checking her over. "Thanks to Gloria."

"Mmmm." Nancy walked slowly around the stall, her gaze trained on the ground, looking for clues. "So tell me about Gloria. How come she has to braid horses at three A.M. while the owners get their beauty sleep?"

Colleen sighed as she took down the hay net and started stuffing hay into it. "That's some story. Three years ago Gloria was at the top. She even won a silver medal at the 1988 Olympic Games. Then she decided to go professional and was riding for a dozen different owners. It seemed as if she was in every show. She'd fly from the West Coast to the East Coast in one week. It was crazy—she was obsessed with winning."

"Is she like that now?" Nancy asked. Stooping down next to the stall door, she began hunting through the straw.

"No. I think she learned her lesson." Colleen hung up the hay net, then went out to get a brush. When she returned, she went on. "Last year at the Washington International, Gloria was determined to break the indoor high-jump record. The horse she was riding was fairly young, and he fell during the jump-off."

"Was Gloria hurt?"

Colleen nodded. "She broke her back and was in the hospital for months. But what really messed up her career was the fact that the owners of the horse had told her *not* to ride in the jump-off. Gloria didn't listen. The horse soured after his fall, and they had to start all over again with his training. The owners made a big stink about it. Nothing happened legally, but when

Gloria was well enough to ride again, no one wanted to take a chance with her."

"Except you."

Colleen shrugged. "That's different. She wouldn't be riding my horse. She'd be training me."

"So what's she doing now?"

"Oh, she runs a small stable and gives clinics and lessons. Most of her students ride in hunter classes."

"So that's why she's so eager to work with you and Nightingale," Nancy mused.

"Yeah. It would get her into big-time jumping again."

"Hmmm. It seems like everyone has an interesting story."

Colleen looked puzzled. "What do you mean?"

"Yesterday Scott was telling me about his horse— Hey! What's this?" Nancy peered at a fuzzy blue fiber that was caught on a splinter on the side of the stall door.

"Colleen," Nancy said in a low voice. "Take a look at this."

Colleen squatted next to her. Carefully Nancy pulled the fiber free and held it up for her friend to see.

"Looks like yarn," Colleen said.

Nancy nodded. "Right. And if my hunch is correct, it's the same blue yarn that Marisa San Marcos was braiding into her horse's mane!"

10

Bound for Trouble

"First the mask, now the yarn," Colleen said, frowning. "I'd say that's plenty of proof that the San Marcoses are up to no good. Maybe I was wrong about them wanting Nightingale. Maybe the only thing they want is to see her out of the show."

Nancy was ready to agree. But a little voice inside was telling her that, twice now, the physical evidence had been too easy to find. "Unless someone planted the yarn to *make* them look guilty," Nancy said slowly.

"What are you guys doing grubbing around in the straw?" a deep voice said above them.

"Phil!" Colleen jumped to her feet. "I thought you were going to study."

"Nah." Phil ran his fingers through his dark hair. "Maybe I'll try after lunch."

As Nancy slowly stood up, she casually checked Phil out. His hair was still wet from a shower, and his dark eyes were wide awake. He didn't look as though he'd been up half the night to let out the horse, but still . . .

"So what's with Sleeping Beauty?" With a grin Phil pointed into the extra stall. Bess was curled up in a tight ball, a silly smile on her face.

"I'd say she was dreaming about Prince Charming," Nancy said with a laugh. She went in to wake up her friend while Colleen told Phil about Nightingale getting loose.

"Ummm." Bess sat up and stretched. "I slept great." When she saw Colleen and Phil talking in the doorway, she stopped in midstretch. "What time is it, anyway? You guys look like you've been up for hours."

"It's eight. Time for breakfast," Nancy told her. She looked back at Phil, trying to read his expression as Colleen finished telling him about Nightingale almost escaping through the open gate. His mouth was set in a grim line.

Colleen turned to Nancy and Bess. "You two need to get something to eat," she urged. "Phil and I will take over. I'm going to give Nightingale a light workout, then a bath."

"Bath." Bess groaned. "That sounds wonderful."

Colleen tossed Nancy the truck keys and the key to the motel room. "Your suitcases are in two-oh-six. And don't use all the hot water," she added with a laugh.

Three hours later Nancy was at the warm-up ring, watching Colleen school Nightingale over several of the practice jumps. A dozen ponies and their young riders were waiting by the arena gate for the next competition to begin.

Earlier, Nancy and Bess had showered, changed, and eaten a late breakfast. Bess had decided to hit the shops on the concourse again. Nancy wanted to keep her eye on Nightingale.

As Nancy watched, Nightingale trotted past and Colleen waved. The mare's chestnut coat gleamed, and her white socks sparkled. As she cantered around the ring, her ears were pricked eagerly. Her strides were so smooth and light that she seemed to be floating.

Nancy held her breath as Colleen turned Nightingale toward a high set of poles. Without hesitation, the mare boldly took off. Tucking her front legs tight against her chest, she cleared the fence by a foot.

"If she had wings, she could fly," a voice said next to Nancy. She looked to her left. Scott Weller was beside her, astride a tall gray horse. His gaze was glued to Nightingale as the mare took two more jumps.

"Hi." Nancy smiled. "And who's this you're riding?"

Scott patted the tall, solid gray. "This is the Stanleys' horse, Wintergreen. He's a Dutch Warmblood." He grinned when he noticed Nancy's confusion. "That's a breed. Amsterdam isn't just famous for their tulips."

Nancy laughed. "Wintergreen's a big guy."

"Talented, too." Scott affectionately whacked the gray's rump, but his brows were knotted in a frown. "He'll have to be, to beat Nightingale."

"Are you worried?" Nancy asked, looking up at him. But Scott's attention was on Colleen and her horse. He didn't seem to hear Nancy.

"Scott?" Nancy repeated.

"Hmmm?" Scott looked back at her as if he'd just noticed she was there.

"You seem kind of worried about the class."

"No. I guess I was off on my usual cloud—wondering what it will be like when I finally own my own horse again."

"I take it you don't like riding for other people," Nancy said.

Scott shrugged. "The money's good. But the owner or trainer or somebody is always telling you what to do." Nancy saw momentary sparks of anger dance in his eyes.

Scott continued. "If I had my own horse—like Nightingale for instance—I could take her straight to the top. Colleen's a good rider, but that mare needs someone who has the drive and determination to go all the way." His last words were spoken in a terse voice, and Nancy noticed that Scott was again staring intently at the chestnut mare.

"And that person could be you?" she asked softly. But before Scott could answer, Colleen trotted over and dismounted.

"Whoooo. She did great!" Colleen said happily.

"She looked great, too," Nancy said, glancing at Scott. The anger had left his face, and once more he was smiling charmingly. Nancy couldn't help but wonder what was going on in Scott's mind.

"Hey, Weller," Phil Ackerman said in a gruff voice as he approached the group, "don't you have anything better to do than hang around my girlfriend?"

Scott shot him a look of disgust. "And don't you have anything better to do than spy on her?"

"Hey, guys," Colleen interjected, a note of anger in her voice, "knock it off."

Nancy stepped back to observe the three of them. Something was obviously going on that Colleen hadn't told her about. But before Nancy could think of what it might be, Marisa San Marcos rushed over.

"Colleen, Nightingale looked sensational!" the young girl exclaimed. She threw her arms around Nightingale's neck and gave the mare a squeeze. "You're going to be tough to beat in the Worthington Cup."

"Oh, I bet you'll give me a run for my money," Colleen said.

"Marisa!" a stern voice boomed over the exercise ring. Nancy turned to see Diego San Marcos standing in the middle of the stable entryway, holding Mr. Sunshine. He had a frown on his face. "You have work to do."

"Gotta go. Bye!" Marisa waved her fingers cheerily and bounced away, as if her father's stern voice didn't bother her in the least. If Marisa was responsible for Nightingale's injuries, Nancy thought, she sure was good at hiding it.

"I'd better get moving, too," Scott said. "That is, if I'm going to beat you in the Gambler's Choice tonight." Flashing Colleen a grin, he jogged his horse into the warm-up ring.

Phil took the reins from Colleen. "Come on. I'll help you bathe Nightingale."

Nancy caught Colleen's arm before she could walk away. "I need to talk to you," she said in a low voice. She wanted to ask Colleen more about Scott, and why Phil was acting so jealous around him. Maybe Phil's behavior had nothing to do with Nightingale. Then again, maybe it did.

Colleen nodded. "Later," she whispered. Then she followed Phil from the warm-up ring.

For a few minutes Nancy watched Marisa school Mr. Sunshine. The young girl was definitely a talented rider. She was quiet and confident, light and easy on her horse, yet she seemed to be able to push Mr. Sunshine to jump higher and higher as Diego raised the poles.

"What's up?" Bess said at Nancy's elbow. She was sipping a soda and snacking from a bag of cashews.

Nancy shook her head. "I'm just thinking about Marisa. Her enthusiasm and love for Nightingale seem genuine. Maybe that's why I can't picture her as our culprit."

"Yeah. I know what you mean." Bess offered Nancy some cashews. "I can't say the same for her father, though. I still think he'd do anything to win."

Nancy's gaze shifted to Diego. He was smacking a riding crop against his tall boots. "Not good enough!" he shouted at Marisa.

"You're probably right," Nancy answered. "The question is, would he be careless enough to leave both the yarn and the mask behind to incriminate his own daughter? Somehow, I don't think so."

Bess stopped chewing. "So we're back to Phil again?"

Nancy told her about the words between Phil and Scott. "I'm not sure Colleen's told us everything," she said as they started back to the stable area. "I'd like to talk to her again."

But when they finally found Colleen, she and Phil were washing Nightingale outside. Nancy and Bess got busy cleaning and oiling the saddle and bridle. At five-thirty they all had a quick dinner before Colleen went into the show ring to walk the course before the Gambler's Choice. She had to decide in which order to jump the obstacles to rack up the maximum number of points.

"Well, this is it," Phil said to Nancy as she wiped Nightingale's coat with a damp rag. He was kneeling on the concrete, brushing gloss on the mare's hooves. Bess had gone out to the truck to get Colleen's riding outfit.

"All this work and preparation for just one class," he added with a snort.

"It is a lot of work," Nancy admitted.

"Now do you see why I'd do anything to convince Colleen to get out of showing?" he asked, pausing to look up at her.

Nancy wondered what Phil meant by *anything*. She'd already seen several examples of his jealous nature. How far would he go to have Colleen all to himself?

"Anything?" she queried in a light voice.

He threw Nancy a stony look. Then, without a word, he bent down to brush gloss on Nightingale's back hooves. Nancy wondered about his reaction to her question. Was he feeling guilty?

"I think I've got everything." Bess came up the aisle with two hangers in her hand. At the same time, Colleen headed back from the other direction.

94

"Wow. That course is tough," she grumbled, frown lines etched in her forehead. "Tight and tricky. The jumps with the highest points have spreads that must be six feet wide."

Phil stood up. "Hey, you can always back out."

Colleen shook her head. "No way. This show's going to prove whether Nightingale's really got it." She patted the mare's neck. "Well, I'd better get dressed. I spent so much time on the course, I'm running late."

"We'll tack up Nightingale." Nancy already had the bridle in her hand.

Bess picked up Colleen's well-shined boots. "And I'll give you a hand, Colleen."

"Thanks, guys." Colleen flashed them all a grateful smile, then followed Bess into the spare stall. Nancy bridled Nightingale, carefully checking all the straps and buckles. In silence Phil picked up the saddle and lightly tossed it onto the mare's back. He tightened the girth, then wiped the saddle off one last time.

"Ready, Colleen?" he hollered into the spare stall.

"I'm missing my stock pin," Colleen called back. "I think it's in the glove compartment of the truck."

"I'll get it," Bess volunteered. She started briskly down the aisle, then turned back, a confused expression on her face. "What's a stock pin?"

"It's a big pin you put in your choker." She pointed to the white band around her neck. "It secures it to your shirt." Seeing Bess's bewilderment, Colleen laughed. "Never mind. I'll run out and get it, then meet you guys at the warm-up ring. That way I can use the truck mirror to pin it on straight." Grabbing her hunt cap, she hurried down the aisle.

Fifteen minutes later Bess, Nancy, and Nightingale were waiting at the warm-up ring. Nancy was holding the mare. Phil had headed for the main arena, which was filled with spectators, saying he was going to find a good spot to take pictures. Colleen hadn't shown up.

"I wonder where she is," Nancy said, checking her watch. The Gambler's Choice had started. Two riders had already completed the course. Nightingale was beginning to get excited as horses galloped and jumped around her. She chewed on her rein and pranced in a circle.

"Easy, girl." Nancy tried to calm the mare down, but she was starting to get nervous herself. If Colleen didn't hurry, she'd miss the class.

"I'm going to look for Colleen," Nancy said finally.

"And leave me with Nightingale?" Bess squeaked. Nancy understood her friend's hesitation. The mare was getting more and more restless.

Just then Nancy saw Phil coming down the

steps from the concourse. "Phil can help," she said. Catching his eye, she waved him over. Before he reached them, she thrust the reins into Bess's hands. "I've got to hurry. Can you handle her until he gets here?"

"Well, I guess," Bess said as Nancy took off at a run for the stable area.

Taking a right, Nancy found the fastest route to the parking lot. Her heart was pounding. A nagging fear told her that Colleen wouldn't be this late unless something was wrong.

When she reached the truck, it was dark and empty. Either Colleen had never made it to the truck, or she'd already gotten the stock pin and locked it back up. Nancy paused, trying to figure out where to look next for her friend. Back at Nightingale's stall?

Just then she heard a muffled grunt from the horse trailer. Nancy held her breath but didn't hear anything. Had she imagined it? But then she detected a thud, like something hitting the trailer wall.

Without a second thought Nancy sprinted to the trailer and swung open the door. The light from the parking lot streamed into the front part of the trailer. It was empty, except for a bale of hay.

Nancy stepped inside. "Colleen?" she called urgently. Hearing a muffled noise, Nancy ducked under the partition that went in front of the horse's chest. It was then that she saw her friend.

Colleen was lying on her side, shoved against the wheel well. Her mouth was taped shut. Her wrists and feet had been tied together with the stretchy bandages used to wrap horses' legs, and her eyes were wide with fear.

11

A Dangerous Challenge

"Colleen!" Nancy dropped to the rubber mat covering the floor. Colleen's eyes lit up with relief when she saw her.

"Let me get this off you," Nancy said as she slowly unpeeled the tape from her friend's mouth. "What happened?" she asked.

"I don't know," Colleen replied in a trembling voice. "Somebody in a black mask and cape jumped me from behind when I was leaning into the truck." She shivered. "It happened so fast, I didn't get a good look at the person."

"The caped intruder has struck again," Nancy said grimly.

Colleen nodded toward her hands. "Quick, untie me. I've got to get into the arena in time to ride." Her eyes flashed angrily. "Whoever did this isn't going to have the satisfaction of seeing me miss the class."

"That's the spirit." Nancy removed the wraps that bound her friend's wrists.

"I almost had my legs untied," Colleen said, as she and Nancy undid the bandages around her boots. "Whoever it was seemed to be in a big hurry."

Nancy helped Colleen to her feet. "Ooo," Colleen said, grimacing. "If I'd stayed in that position much longer, I'd really be stiff."

As the two girls climbed from the trailer, Nancy said, "I'll close it up. You hightail it in there."

Nancy kept an eye on Colleen until her friend had disappeared into the stable area. Then, after throwing shut the latch on the trailer door, she followed her.

By the time Nancy reached the warm-up ring, Colleen was in the saddle. Nancy was surprised to see Gloria Donner holding the mare's bridle. With a look of determination, Colleen stuck her feet into the stirrups. Then, squeezing Nightingale with her heels, she urged the mare into a trot.

"Colleen's next!" Bess said excitedly when Nancy jogged up.

"Our next rider is Colleen Healey, on Nightingale," the loudspeaker blasted. Colleen cantered past the two girls. Her face was flushed, and she looked straight ahead.

The wooden gate opened into the arena. A big

bay horse trotted out, and Colleen and Nightingale trotted in.

"Where's Phil?" Nancy whispered to Bess as they ran up the steps to watch Colleen jump. "And what was Gloria Donner doing holding Nightingale?"

"Phil left to find you," Bess said. "He thought you'd both gotten lost in the parking lot. But I couldn't handle Nightingale any longer. She'd gotten half crazy. So Phil gave her to Gloria." Bess took a breath. The short set of stairs had led them to the bottom aisle that circled the arena. Above them were row after row of seats and the exits into the main concourse.

Nancy glanced around, wondering who could have tied up Colleen. She could see Phil on the opposite side of the arena, holding a camera to his eye. Phil had disappeared after they'd first reached the warm-up ring. Had he run outside, taped up Colleen, and tossed her into the trailer? He'd been the only suspect who knew she was headed out to the truck. And he hadn't been too eager to see her ride.

Or had someone else noticed Colleen going outside into the dark night? Had someone grabbed the leg wraps and sneaked out after her? Then it had to have been done on the spur of the moment, Nancy reasoned. There was no way the culprit could have known that Colleen would go out to the truck right before her class.

"Where did you find Colleen?" Bess asked when she and Nancy had found seats in the front row.

"I'll tell you later," Nancy whispered. The buzzer had sounded, and Colleen was steering Nightingale toward the first jump.

Nancy crossed her fingers. Colleen hadn't had time to warm up with Nightingale, and Nancy knew her friend was shaken. Would it affect her performance? When Nightingale galloped past, Nancy could see that Colleen's lips were pressed together tensely. But the mare jumped the first obstacle without a hitch. Then, ears pricked as if she were enjoying herself, Nightingale made a tight turn and leapt through an in and out. Nancy smiled with relief.

Twisting, turning, jumping like a deer, Nightingale made it through the course without touching a pole. Only moments later the buzzer sounded, and horse and rider galloped to the finish line.

"What a round!" the announcer exclaimed above the sound of the spectators' applause and cheering. "With a total of one hundred seventy-five points, that's the highest score so far. But we have one more rider—Scott Weller, on Wintergreen. Let's see if he can beat Colleen Healey's score."

Colleen and Nightingale trotted out just as Scott cantered in on the big gray. Bess stood up, ready to go downstairs and congratulate Colleen.

Nancy put her hand on her arm. "Let's watch Scott first."

While Scott trotted his horse in a circle, Nancy looked up into the seats. Her gaze traveled around the arena until she spotted Diego and Marisa. They were just entering a private sky suite. Diego immediately stepped to the edge when Scott's name was announced and watched the horse and rider's round with a look of concern. Marisa sat down and began sipping a soda.

Nancy frowned. "Did you see either Marisa or Diego in the warm-up ring?"

Bess thought for a moment. "No. Why?"

"Their stalls are located in the aisle that leads to the parking lot. I'm wondering if they saw Colleen leave the stable area, followed her, and tied her up."

Bess gasped. "Colleen was tied up?"

Nancy nodded. "Someone wanted her to miss this class."

"But Marisa's not even riding in it. What would she gain?"

"I don't know. That's what makes it puzzling."

The buzzer rang, and Nancy's attention was drawn back to Scott on the powerful gray. He was galloping Wintergreen around the course at breakneck speed.

Nancy heard Bess draw in her breath. "He's going to fall!" Bess said. "I just know it."

"Let's hope not," Nancy reassured her friend.

"Scott realizes that he's got to beat Nightingale's time in order to win."

The buzzer rang again, and the big gray charged for the finish line.

"One hundred and seventy-five points, folks," the announcer said gleefully above the excited crowd. "Looks like we have a tie!"

Nancy stood up. "I'm going to see if Colleen's all right. Why don't you stay here and save our seats?"

She dashed downstairs to the warm-up area. Colleen had dismounted and was leading Nightingale in a small circle. Gloria Donner was walking next to her.

"I don't know." Colleen was shaking her head. "I just feel that, since Nightingale did her best, once was enough. I'll tell the ringmaster I'm not going to participate in the jump-off."

"No way! Nightingale jumped that course as though the fences were all two feet high," Gloria replied. "She's more than ready. And remember, first place is a thousand bucks more. That buys a lot of feed."

Just then Scott rode up. "Well, Colleen?" he said, flashing a challenging grin. "Should we make this a repeat of the Columbia Classic?"

Colleen's head snapped back as she looked up at Scott. Her fingers gripped the reins tight, and Nancy could see the hesitation in her eyes. Nancy wondered what Scott meant. At the same time she was thinking that Gloria was right. Nightingale *had* breezed around the course. Why was Colleen so reluctant for a jump-off?

"Oh, Colleen, you're going to win! I just know it!" Marisa came bounding up with her usual enthusiastic greeting. Throwing one arm over the saddle, she gave Nightingale a hug.

At the same time a bright flash of light flashed in everyone's eyes.

"Got you," Phil said from behind his camera. "A winner." He nodded toward Colleen. "And a loser." He smiled nastily at Scott. "Side by side in the same photo. Maybe the newspapers will buy it."

"Except the winner's going to be Wintergreen," Scott shot back as he rode off.

"Go for it, Colleen," Gloria said in a firm voice. She'd been standing next to Marisa on the right side of Nightingale. Passing around the mare's rear, she laced her fingers together to offer Colleen a leg up.

Colleen hesitated for a moment, then smiled. "Oh, all right."

She set her knee in Gloria's cupped hands, and the older woman swung her onto the horse. Colleen gathered her reins. Without a backward glance, she trotted Nightingale into the ring.

Nancy ran upstairs to rejoin Bess.

"Is it just my imagination, or does Colleen look really nervous?" Bess asked in a low voice.

"It's not just your imagination," Nancy replied. "I think Gloria Donner kind of talked her

into the jump-off. Colleen would have been happy with second place."

The two girls fell silent as the buzzer rang once
again. Colleen steered Nightingale over the first
jump, then made an abrupt U-turn toward a
triple oxer—the highest fence, worth the most
points.

"I'm not going to look," Bess said, covering her
eyes.

Nancy held her breath. Suddenly Colleen and
the saddle slipped sideways. There was an audi-
ble gasp from the audience. Colleen grabbed
Nightingale's braided mane, trying to keep herself upright. At the same time Nightingale, sens-
ing something was wrong, slid to an abrupt stop.

Like a launched missile, Colleen flew headfirst
over Nightingale's head and crashed into the
jump, scattering the heavy poles as if they were
twigs.

12

A Sudden Realization

"Colleen's hurt!" Bess cried.

Without a second's hesitation Nancy rushed down the steps, vaulted the arena wall, and ran through the tanbark to where Colleen was lying. Her friend's eyes were shut and her body was very still. Nancy moved a pole that had fallen on Colleen's leg, then took her friend's wrist in her hand. Colleen's pulse was normal.

"Colleen!" Phil knelt next to Nancy. "Is she alive?" he asked in a voice choking with pain.

Nancy nodded. An official ran over just as the rescue vehicle roared through the gate. "Don't move her," the official said in a tense voice.

Looking up briefly, Nancy scanned the arena for Nightingale. The mare had jogged to the other end of the ring, reins dragging in the tanbark. The saddle had slipped halfway down her side. Nancy could see Gloria Donner, lead line in hand, approaching the frightened horse. The spectators were all standing to get a better look and murmuring among themselves.

Two medics pushed past Phil and stopped on either side of Colleen. Nancy stood up and stepped back. Phil stayed by Colleen's head, his hand gripping hers.

"It's good she was wearing a hard hat," one of the medics muttered. "Blood pressure's low. Nothing seems to be broken, but you never know."

Carefully they unsnapped Colleen's hunt cap and pulled it off her head. "No visible contusions or cuts," the other medic said. "Let's strap her on the stretcher and take her to the hospital."

"I'm going with her," Phil said in a firm voice.

Nancy nodded. "We'll take care of Nightingale. I'll call as soon as I can."

Bess came up as the medics slid Colleen into the back of the rescue vehicle. Phil climbed in after her. Sitting down, he took Colleen's hand and pressed it to his lips. There were tears in his eyes.

The medics closed the double doors, and Nancy and Bess silently watched the rescue vehicle leave. Then Nancy turned toward Gloria Donner, who was leading Nightingale toward them. She'd taken the saddle off so it wasn't hanging under the still-nervous mare.

"I'm really sorry," Gloria said in a hushed

voice. Her face was pale and her mouth drawn. "Do they think Colleen will be okay?"

Nancy took Nightingale's reins and slowly started to lead the mare to the gate. "There don't seem to be any broken bones, but it's hard to tell at this point."

Gloria shook her head as she walked along beside them. "This brings back bad memories. At least Nightingale's okay. And she had sense enough to stop before the jump. Otherwise, it could have been a real mess."

A real mess is right, Nancy thought. I should have known something like this was going to happen. And I should have been able to prevent it somehow. Nancy sighed in frustration.

"So what do you think happened?" Bess asked.

"I'd say that, in all the confusion before the jump-off, Colleen forgot to check her girth," Gloria answered. "As a horse exercises, you usually need to raise the strap a notch. A simple fact, but if you don't, the saddle could easily slip, and . . ." Her voice trailed off as they went through the gate.

"Is Colleen all right?" Scott jogged up on Wintergreen, his eyes wide with concern.

"We don't know," Bess said solemnly.

The loudspeaker blasted something about Colleen, then Scott's name. He flushed. "What a way to win the class," he muttered. With an apologetic smile he trotted Wintergreen into the ring to receive his trophy.

"Hey, you guys." Gloria turned to Nancy and Bess. "My three girls aren't riding until tomorrow morning. I'd be happy to help with Nightingale."

"That's okay," Nancy replied. "I think we can handle it."

"At least let me walk her for a while," Gloria insisted, "to make sure she's not hurt."

"That's a good idea, Nancy," Bess said. "Especially since we don't know much about horse injuries."

"All right," Nancy finally agreed. Gloria seemed sincere. But right now she didn't want *anyone* handling Nightingale except her and Bess. Too much had happened already. Even though it might have been an accident—in all the excitement and confusion, Colleen might have forgotten to tighten Nightingale's girth— Nancy wanted to be extra cautious.

In silence Nancy, Bess, and Gloria walked to the stable area. Nancy held tightly to Nightingale's lead. Even the mare seemed quiet, as if she knew something was wrong.

"I'll put the saddle away," Gloria offered.

"There's a saddle rack in the extra stall," Bess said.

When Gloria went in, Bess reached out and ran her hand down Nightingale's white blaze. "I sure hope Colleen's okay," she said to Nancy in a low voice. "When I signed up for bodyguard duty, I thought I was going to protect a horse. I wasn't figuring on Colleen getting hurt."

110

Nancy frowned. "I know how you feel. Here, hold Nightingale while I get her halter, okay?"

She handed the reins to Bess, then walked into the extra stall. Gloria had set the saddle down on the rack and was standing on the far side of it. She'd lifted the flap of leather the rider's leg rested against and was peering underneath.

When she saw Nancy, Gloria's face flushed as if she'd been caught with her hand in a cookie jar. "Uh, just running up the stirrups," she said quickly.

"Thanks," Nancy murmured, keeping her eyes on the older woman. With a strained smile Gloria dropped the leather panel and stepped around the rack.

"I'll check Nightingale's legs now," she said, and strode from the stall without looking at Nancy.

Now what was all that about? Nancy wondered. She knew Gloria wasn't running up the stirrups on the stirrup straps. They'd already been secured before they'd left the ring. It was very unlikely that a stirrup had slipped down again.

Curious, Nancy walked around to the other side of the saddle. She lifted the panel and checked underneath. There were two straps that were fastened under the horse's belly. Each strap had a buckle on either side. One set of buckles was unfastened each time the saddle was removed. The other set of buckles remained fastened at the same place, and these holes had

111

become worn with use. Studying the girth, Nancy immediately noticed that it had been lowered one notch below the two worn holes where Colleen normally buckled the straps. Nancy remembered, because she'd been careful to rebuckle the girth at the two worn holes when she'd cleaned it earlier. Then she'd double-checked the tightness with Colleen.

A chill ran over Nancy as she dropped the leather flap. So Colleen's fall definitely wasn't an accident. Grabbing the halter, she darted back into the aisle. She had some questions to ask Gloria Donner.

But the older woman wasn't there.

"Where's Gloria?" Nancy asked Bess.

"She left," Bess replied, startled. "What's going on?"

Nancy threw her friend the halter. "No time to explain," she said as she took off toward the stalls where she'd first met Gloria. But the trainer wasn't there, either.

Nancy approached a young girl brushing a bay horse. "Have you seen Gloria Donner?" Nancy asked her.

"She just left a minute ago," the girl replied. "I think she yelled something about a late dinner."

"Where's she staying? What motel?" Nancy insisted.

The girl stopped brushing and gave her a strange look.

"Please, it's important."

"Holiday House."

Nancy dashed for the parking lot. She still had the truck keys in her pocket. But once outside, she changed her mind. Gloria Donner obviously knew something. She'd acted too suspicious when Nancy had caught her looking at the girth. But leaving Bess alone with Nightingale was too risky.

As Nancy walked back into the stable area, she recalled seeing Gloria on Nightingale's right side before Colleen had gone in for the jump-off. And Gloria had been holding Nightingale right before the class. That meant the trainer had had ample opportunity to lower the girth when no one was looking. But why would Gloria Donner have done such a thing?

Was she working with Diego San Marcos? Had he offered her money or a job in return for sabotaging Colleen's ride?

Nancy broke into a jog, quickly reaching Nightingale's stall. Bess had untacked the mare and was buckling on the halter.

"Hey, you're getting good at this." Nancy grinned at her friend, relieved to see that both Bess and Nightingale were all right.

Bess patted Nightingale on the neck. "That's because I have a horse who knows I need a lot of cooperation." Then her expression turned serious. "So are you going to tell me what that was all about?"

"I'm pretty sure someone loosened Nightingale's girth before Colleen went in for the jump-off."

"What?" Bess's mouth dropped open. "You mean it wasn't an accident?"

"I don't think so," Nancy answered. "And I have a feeling Gloria Donner's in on it."

"Gloria? You wondered about her before—the night Nightingale got out." Bess frowned, puzzled. "But why would she want to hurt Colleen and Nightingale's chances to win? Doesn't she want to be their trainer?"

Nancy sighed. "Good questions. Maybe the woman's just really ambitious. Colleen told us that Gloria was obsessed with winning before her accident."

Bess shook her head. "But she also said she thought Gloria had changed."

"Maybe that's what Gloria wants everyone to think," Nancy replied. "Maybe somebody's offering her something in exchange for her help."

"Like what? And who?"

Brows furrowed in thought, Nancy walked to Nightingale's side. She wished she had a definite answer or more evidence. Then maybe she could alert the arena's security force.

"Nightingale's kind of sweaty," Nancy said, patting the mare's wet neck. "I'd better wash her off and walk her awhile. Why don't you call the hospital and see if there's any news?"

"Okay," Bess agreed. "Are you sure you'll be all right?"

114

Nancy smiled confidently. "Oh, sure. Just let someone try and get to Nightingale. They'll never get past me."

"Go get 'em." Bess gave Nancy the thumbs-up sign, then grabbed her purse and went to find a pay phone.

After her friend had left, Nancy picked up a bucket and led Nightingale outside to the water spigots. A half-dozen other grooms and riders were washing their horses. Nancy recognized several riders from the Gambler's Choice. All of them asked about Colleen.

Nancy told them she didn't have any news yet. Then she filled up the bucket with soapy water. As she scrubbed Nightingale's back, Nancy was lost in thought. How could Gloria Donner be involved? she wondered. All of the physical evidence so far, as well as a possible motive, pointed to the San Marcoses.

Suddenly Nancy stopped scrubbing. Marisa had also been on Nightingale's right side before Colleen had gone into the jump-off. Had she lowered the girth? Had Gloria seen her? Maybe the trainer wasn't guilty after all. Maybe she'd just been checking the saddle to see for herself if someone had tampered with the girth.

Maybe. But then why had Gloria acted so guilty? At least the girth incident had pushed Phil into the background, Nancy thought. Or had it?

Phil could have lowered the girth much earlier,

thinking that the saddle would slip just enough to throw horse and rider off-balance. Only then his plan had backfired, and Colleen had fallen. Nancy knew Phil Ackerman wanted his girlfriend to quit riding, but she didn't think he'd deliberately hurt Colleen.

Deliberately hurt Colleen. Nancy repeated the words to herself. Suddenly her hand holding the sponge froze in midair once again. That's what she'd been missing. Until tonight, all the attempts had been on Nightingale. Nancy had always assumed it was the horse the culprits were after.

But now that she knew the loosened girth had been no accident, Nancy had to rethink everything. She thought back to all the things done to Nightingale—the blister, the poisoned hay, letting the mare loose.

None of those things had really hurt Nightingale, of course. Even the bouncing bet thrown in the hay had been just toxic enough to give the mare a stomachache. But Colleen's fall was serious—deadly serious. Whoever was behind all of this wasn't out to harm Nightingale. Someone was now after Colleen.

13

True Confessions

"Nancy, I got through to the hospital." Bess came rushing up, a big grin on her face.

"How's Colleen feeling?" Nancy asked, her earlier thoughts pushed aside for now.

"She regained consciousness on the way to the hospital," Bess said. "They're taking X rays, but Phil says the doctors don't think she has any broken bones."

"Whew. That's good news. Things might have been worse." Nancy's voice was solemn as she rinsed Nightingale with the hose.

"I know that look you've got on your face," Bess said. "You've figured something out. Are you going to let me in on it?"

"Yup." Nancy turned and pointed to the bucket. "First, hand me the scraper."

Bess reached down and handed Nancy the

long, scooped piece of metal used to whisk excess water off the horse's coat.

"Well?" Bess prompted.

Nancy glanced around to make sure no one was listening. "All this time we've been protecting Nightingale because we thought she was the target."

Bess nodded in agreement.

"But when you look back at all the things that happened to her, she never really got hurt. Not seriously, anyway."

Bess shrugged. "Okay, so maybe our bad guys bungled the job."

"Four times?"

Bess screwed up her face. "Yeah. I see your point. But maybe the culprits got desperate, which is why Colleen got hurt. Her accident today will probably keep both of them from competing in tomorrow's Worthington Cup, right?"

As she dried the mare's face, Nancy thought for a moment. "Could be. But I think our mystery person wants Nightingale safe and sound. In fact, I think the person wants Nightingale so bad, he or she will do anything to get her."

"Do you think Marisa would hurt Colleen just to get Nightingale?" Bess asked.

"Well, think about it. If Colleen had been seriously injured, she'd definitely have to sell Nightingale. Right now her winnings are the only thing that's paying for feed. And who would exercise Nightingale?" Nancy leaned down to dump out the bucket. "But that doesn't necessarily narrow it down to Marisa," she went on. "Phil would be ecstatic if Colleen quit riding."

"Nancy!" Bess sounded shocked. "I don't know how you can accuse him. Phil was in tears when Colleen fell."

Nancy snorted. "If he'd been the cause of her fall, he *should* have been in tears."

Bess put her hands on her hips. "Phil really loves Colleen, Nancy, and you know it."

Nancy didn't respond. Picking up the bucket again, she began to lead Nightingale into the stable area. Bess trudged along beside her.

"Then there's Gloria's strange behavior, and Scott . . ." Nancy mused aloud, her voice trailing off.

"Scott? How did he get dragged into this?" Bess asked. "I swear, Nancy, I think you're ready to accuse everyone and anyone."

Nancy chuckled at her friend's indignation, thinking that Bess should know that she had to view everyone as a potential suspect.

"You may be right," Nancy conceded as they walked down the aisle. "In fact, I wouldn't be surprised if we have two suspects, with two different motives."

"As I said before, this case gets curiouser and curiouser," Bess said with a sigh.

* * *

Twenty minutes later Nightingale was settled in her stall, munching hay. Nancy and Bess had set up their cots and were wearily slumped on them. It was ten o'clock, and both girls were exhausted.

For a while Nancy tried to think about the case, but then she closed her eyes—just for a minute, she told herself. The next thing she knew, someone was shaking her shoulder.

"Nancy!" The voice was urgent. "I've got to talk to you." Nancy recognized Phil Ackerman's voice.

Instantly her eyes flew open, and she sat up on the cot. It was still dark out. She looked at her watch and noticed she'd been asleep for only a few minutes. "What? What's wrong? Is Colleen okay?"

Phil nodded, then motioned to the aisle. "Come on out here. I don't want to wake up Bess."

Nancy swung her legs to the side of the cot and stuck her feet in her sneakers. Then she pulled a sweatshirt over her head and stood up. For a moment she thought about waking Bess. It was late and the barn was quiet. What if Phil was planning to bop her on the head?

Nancy scoffed at her own idea. Not only was she prepared to defend herself, but she didn't think Phil would try anything. He probably just had news about Colleen.

She stepped out into the aisle. Phil was seated

on a hay bale, his head propped in his hands. When Nancy approached, he looked up. His smile seemed strained and tired.

"Is Colleen—?"

He held up his hand to silence her question. "She's fine. She's back at the motel, sleeping like a baby. The doctor released her, saying she needed to take it easy for a few days. I called her parents. They said they'd be here in the morning." He sighed. "She's insisting on riding in the Worthington Cup."

"Well, we just won't let her," Nancy said firmly.

"I was hoping you'd say that." Phil smiled at her again, and Nancy couldn't help but smile back. But then Phil looked awkwardly down at the floor.

"Nancy . . ." Phil began. Then he clenched one hand into a fist and pounded the palm of the other one. "How could I have been so stupid?"

Reaching out, Nancy caught his hand in hers. "Why don't you tell me what you're talking about?" she said gently. "Does it have something to do with the blister?"

Abruptly Phil glanced over at her, his dark eyes wide with pain. "How did you know that?"

"You were at Colleen's that night, you know about things like blisters, and you had a motive."

Phil let out his breath. "That obvious, huh? I guess you know about my letting Nightingale out, too."

121

"You let her out here? At the show?"

"No. No way." Phil shook his head emphatically. "That's why I wanted to talk to you. You probably think I'm involved with what's going on at the show, but I'm not!" His voice rose. "Once Colleen decided to come to the show, I was behind her one hundred percent. I know you think I'm a first-class jerk, but I really do love her and want the best for her. I would *never* do anything to hurt Colleen."

"Then you were the one who let Nightingale out at Colleen's barn?" Nancy asked.

"Right. But I didn't poison her hay!" he insisted. "That would have been going too far."

Nancy frowned. "I thought the blister was going too far."

Phil shook his head. "I only used a little. I thought that if Nightingale wasn't in top form, Colleen wouldn't go to the show. I was afraid if they *did* go, and Nightingale did well, then Colleen would decide not to sell her. If that happened, I knew I'd lose her."

Nancy said nothing.

"At first I thought the poisonous weed in the hay was an accident," Phil continued. "But then, when we got to the show and you found the nails, and someone let Nightingale loose, I realized something fishy was going on. I wanted to talk to you about it earlier. You kept shooting me suspicious looks, so I knew you thought I was the culprit. But we got so busy, and then . . ."

"Colleen fell," Nancy finished his thoughts.

He nodded. Nancy thought Phil's confession sounded sincere. He'd admitted some painful things. And in her heart, she knew Bess was right—Phil may have acted stupidly, but he really did love Colleen. Which meant she needed to concentrate on finding the real culprit.

"Tell me about Scott Weller," Nancy said. It was a question she'd wanted to ask Colleen, but it couldn't wait. "Why is there such hostility between you two?"

Phil shrugged. "Scott and Colleen were dating when I met Colleen. That was also the year his horse had the accident. Colleen assured me that the relationship was breaking up anyway, but Scott still took it hard when Colleen stopped seeing him as a boyfriend."

Nancy frowned. "But he seems so friendly now."

"He got over it, and Colleen went out of her way to be nice to him. She knew he felt pretty bad about his horse. I guess that's what put a strain on the relationship in the first place. Scott just wasn't himself."

Nancy looked at him sharply. "Because of the horse's accident?"

"Yeah. His mare was injured in a jump-off with Colleen at the Columbia Classic. Colleen went on to win the class, as well as high point amateur-owner for the year. Scott acted like that was okay, but he really couldn't handle it."

"Wow. So that's what Scott meant by a repeat performance." Nancy rose and began to pace up and down the aisle. "And it was a repeat performance in more ways than one—only this time Colleen got hurt instead of his horse."

"What are you getting at?" Phil asked.

Nancy stopped in front of Phil. "Scott was never on my suspect list because he didn't seem to have any motive. But now I'm not so sure. He might have the best motive of all—revenge!"

14

Evil on Horseback

Phil shook his head. "Scott's doing so well as a professional rider. Why would he want to risk his whole career just to get back at Colleen? Besides, they were used to competing against each other. Sometimes she'd win, sometimes he'd win."

"I guess you're right," Nancy said slowly. She slumped next to Phil on the hay bale. "And I can't forget about all of the evidence pointing to the San Marcoses. That mask and fiber of yarn were pretty incriminating."

Phil stood up. "Well, I'd better get back to the motel and check on Colleen. I guess I have some explaining to do." He gave Nancy a pained look. "Do you think Colleen will forgive me?"

"Forgive you for what?" a voice asked from down the aisle.

Nancy twisted around. "Colleen?" she said in surprise. "What are you doing here?"

Phil took two giant strides toward her. "You're supposed to be in bed," he said, wrapping a protective arm over her shoulder.

She shrugged it off. "Like an invalid? I feel fine. And I'm riding in the Worthington Cup, no matter what anyone says." Feet firmly planted, hands on hips, Colleen glared at the two of them. "The doctor told me I'm okay, so there's no reason I shouldn't."

"I've got a reason!" Nancy jumped up. "If you ride in the class tomorrow night, it might be the last time you ever get on a horse."

Colleen frowned. "What do you mean?" She looked at Phil, searching for an explanation.

"Nancy's decided it wasn't just Nightingale our culprit was after," Phil said. "It's you, too."

"Me?" Colleen squeaked. "But what about all those terrible things that happened to Nightingale?"

"Uh . . ." Phil glanced nervously over at Nancy.

Nancy looked away, hoping he'd tell Colleen the truth.

"We've got to talk, Colleen," Phil said finally.

Colleen's mouth dropped open as she looked at Phil's flushed face. "So it was you!" Her voice rose in anger. "Nancy was right."

"Colleen, I . . ." Phil reached out and touched her arm. Colleen pulled away from him and marched over to the hay bale. Crossing her arms, she plunked down on the bale.

"At least listen to his explanation," Nancy said, sitting next to her.

Colleen shot Phil a nasty look. "Maybe," she said tersely. "Right now I'm too angry."

Phil let out his breath. "I don't blame you."

There was an awkward silence until Nancy spoke. "Look, I've just thought of a way to catch our culprit. It's about time we turned the tables on him . . . or her," she added.

"Do you think it will work?" Colleen looked hopeful.

Nancy nodded. "I'll bet my life on it." She checked her watch. "It's only ten-thirty. Now, listen carefully. Colleen, you need to walk down the aisles and tell anyone who asks that you're feeling great. So great that you've decided to ride in tomorrow night's costume class."

"But I didn't even register for it," Colleen said, frowning.

"That doesn't matter," Nancy said. "The important thing is to tell everyone that you're going to try out your costume early tomorrow morning. You want to wear it riding Nightingale in the main arena to make sure it doesn't spook her or something."

"You've lost me." Colleen shook her head. "How is that going to catch our culprit?"

"You'll be all alone," Nancy pointed out. "By now our bad guy's getting desperate. He or she will figure this is the last chance to get you."

"Whoa. Hold on a minute." Phil held up both

hands. "I don't like this idea at all. You're using Colleen as bait."

"Not Colleen," Nancy explained. "Me. I'll be dressed in the *Arabian Nights* costume. I'm hoping the person won't know the difference. And I can ride well enough to fool them into thinking it's you—for a little while, anyway. By that time you and the arena security will have nabbed them."

Colleen and Phil looked at each other with doubtful expressions.

"What's going on here?" a sleepy voice called from the extra stall. Bess was standing in the doorway, squinting in the light.

"We're going to catch whoever's after Colleen," Nancy said. "And we're going to need your help."

Bess's eyes snapped instantly awake. "You can count on me!"

"Me, too," Colleen added. "I'm tired of worrying and wondering what's going to happen next."

"Phil?" Nancy looked expectantly at him.

Phil grinned. "I'm with you guys. I just hope I'm the one to catch whoever hurt Colleen."

"Good. Then it's settled." Nancy's eyes twinkled. "Colleen, you and Bess start telling people about the costume class. Phil, you guard Nightingale. I'm going to talk to security personnel. Then I'm going to try on that costume—and see how much I can look like Colleen!"

* * *

"Whoa, Nightingale," Nancy crooned as Bess bent down to give her a leg up. Nancy stuck her knee in Bess's cupped hands, then hoisted herself into Nightingale's saddle. The filmy material from the *Arabian Nights* costume fluttered around Nancy's legs. On her feet she was wearing gold sandals.

Nancy and Bess were standing at the entrance to the main arena. It was five A.M. No one else was around. Phil was already hiding in the arena seats. With his telephoto lens attached to his camera, he was planning to shoot several pictures —just in case the person got away. Despite her protests, Colleen was safely stashed back in the motel. Nancy knew it was too dangerous to have her anywhere on the grounds.

Silently Bess helped Nancy adjust the stirrups. "You be careful," Bess said in a hushed voice. "Especially since those arena security people didn't think much of your idea."

"I can't blame them," Nancy whispered back. "But I think it's the only way. Remember to leave the gate open in case I have to beat a hasty retreat, okay?"

"Right. Then I'll alert security to get into position."

"Don't forget to wait until the last minute," Nancy warned. "I don't want to scare away our bad guys."

Bess nodded.

Nancy reached down and gave her friend's

hand a squeeze. Then she draped the costume's transparent veil across her face and adjusted the scarf over her hair. She wanted to make sure she could be mistaken for Colleen.

Collecting the reins, Nancy urged Nightingale into the main ring with a slight pressure of her calves. Colleen had warned her that the mare was very sensitive.

Nightingale danced forward in an eager trot. The Arabian costume's baggy pants fluttered against the mare's sides. Arching her neck, Nightingale broke into a nervous canter. When the mare spied several pumpkins arranged on a straw bale, she skittered sideways.

"Easy, girl. They're just decorations for Halloween." Nancy glanced up into the seating area. The dim lights from overhead and at the exits cast spooky shadows along the empty rows of seats. Orange and black crepe paper streamers were strung along the railings circling the arena. She couldn't see Phil anywhere.

Then all of Nancy's attention was focused on controlling Nightingale, who snorted and pranced sideways nervously. "I know I'm not Colleen," Nancy told the mare in a reassuring voice. "But I'm trying."

They were almost to the other side of the ring when Nightingale suddenly spun around in alarm. Leaning forward, Nancy grabbed the mare's mane and hung on tight. Something must have startled her, Nancy thought. And then she saw it.

A horse and rider were galloping across the arena—straight toward them! Nancy gasped and pulled Nightingale to a halt. Her heartbeat quickened as she tried to figure out who—or what—it was.

The rider charging toward her had no head or neck. He wore a long black cape, which billowed behind him. In one arm he carried a small, lighted pumpkin, a wicked grin carved in its face.

Nancy's mouth fell open. It was the Headless Horseman!

Or Headless Horsewoman, she thought grimly. Pulling herself together, she sprang into action. Quickly she tightened Nightingale's reins and squeezed the mare's sides with her legs. Nightingale leapt forward and, cantering toward the opposite side of the ring, passed the galloping black horse. Nancy halted Nightingale in the middle of the ring, and with a cry, the Headless Horseman reined the horse to a stop at the far end.

A deep, nasty laugh came from the chest of the horseman. "You can run all you want, Colleen Healey," the voice boomed across the ring in a hoarse cry. "But this time I'm going to get you—for good!"

Great, Nancy thought. The person mistook her for Colleen. Now, if only Nancy could find out who the horseman was. Phil's camera would be useless. Nancy knew she needed to identify the person, in case he or she escaped before security arrived.

As she cantered Nightingale toward the gate, Nancy tried to think of who could be hidden under the Headless Horseman costume. The costume over the person's face muffled the sound, so that Nancy couldn't recognize the deep voice. He or she was a good rider, and slim—probably too slim to be Diego. Was it Marisa under the costume, talking in a disguised voice?

Unfortunately, Nancy didn't recognize the horse. He was chunky and black, and the rider was reining him with one hand as if he were a cow pony.

When Nightingale reached the end of the ring, Nancy quickly checked the gate. Someone had shut it. With a jolt of fear, she noticed that the gate had also been secured with a padlock.

She was trapped!

Nancy's mind raced. Had the horseman locked the gate when she'd first entered the ring? She'd been concentrating on Nightingale and wouldn't have noticed. Or was someone else involved? Someone waiting in the stands? Nancy glanced nervously into the seats, but they still looked empty.

"Oh, hurry up, Bess," Nancy pleaded softly. "Get those security guards down here— pronto."

"Ha! Ha! Ha!" The eerie laugh echoed through the stands. "You'll never get away from me now, Colleen, because I'm the better rider! Nightingale's too good for you. She belongs to me!"

Nancy twirled sideways in her saddle in time to see the Headless Horseman dig his heels into his horse's side. The black horse reared, and with a whoop the two raced toward her across the ring.

Nancy's heart flip-flopped. Quick, think of something, she told herself. Maybe she could jump off Nightingale and escape into the stands. But what if someone was hiding there waiting for her? Besides, she didn't want to leave Nightingale.

Quickly Nancy scanned the seats. Where was Phil? she wondered. Had he double-crossed her?

Nancy took a deep breath. No one was coming to her rescue. She had to get the horseman before he got her. Then she'd find out for sure who it was.

With a racing heart Nancy turned Nightingale so that they faced the charging horse. "Okay, girl. Pretend you're in a jumping class, and it's time to win," Nancy told the mare in as calm a voice as she could manage.

Nightingale's ears twitched, as if she were listening to Nancy. Then they pricked forward as the horseman drew closer. Nancy urged the mare away from the gate, toward the center of the ring and the black apparition racing toward her.

Raising the pumpkin to shoulder level, the

Headless Horseman gave a yell of triumph. Then he threw the pumpkin at Nancy.

"Now!" Nancy leaned forward in the saddle and dug her heels into Nightingale's sides. Startled, the mare leapt into the air. The pumpkin hurtled past, just missing Nancy's head.

At the same time, Nancy grabbed Nightingale's mane with one hand, then reached out and grasped the horseman's flowing back cape with the other. Gritting her teeth, she held on. The jolt almost pulled her off Nightingale, but she held tight to the mare's mane. With all her strength Nancy tore the cape from the rider.

"Ahhh!" The horseman screamed angrily as he was jerked from the saddle. The black horse continued to gallop forward as his rider flew off and landed with a thud in the tanbark. The pumpkin crashed beside him and splattered into several pieces.

"Whoa." Nancy tugged on the reins and turned Nightingale in a circle, halting the mare about fifteen feet from the fallen rider. The horseman's body lay still. All that was left of the pumpkin's carved face grinned wickedly at her.

Nancy shuddered. "Bess? Phil?" she called into the stands. There was no answer. Something must have happened to keep the two of them from coming to her aid.

Slowly Nancy slid from Nightingale's back. When she got closer to the body, she gasped.

Through the dim light she saw a black mask with red sequins staring up at her. Could it be Marisa?

Tears pricked Nancy's eyes. There was no reason for this to have happened, she thought. She and her friends all liked Marisa. Colleen probably could have worked something out with the promising young rider. And now it was too late.

Approaching the body, Nancy noticed that the hair was dark, but to her surprise, it was too short to be Marisa's. Crouching down, Nancy saw that the masked rider was definitely male.

With trembling fingers, Nancy pulled down the mask. Then she gasped once again. The Headless Horseman was Scott Weller!

15

Desperate Choices

"Scott!" Nancy whispered in shock. Her hunch had been right. Colleen's charming, concerned friend must have been putting on an act. All this time he'd been plotting revenge on the rider who'd beaten him in the show at which his horse had been injured.

He'd been so obsessed, he'd almost killed Colleen, Nancy thought angrily. Still, she needed to get him help. With a quick glance at the stands, Nancy saw that they were still empty. Jumping up, she began to lead Nightingale toward the padlocked exit. Maybe if she yelled loud enough, someone would hear her.

"Don't move!" a voice suddenly growled beside her. "It's not over yet."

Nancy whirled to her right. A raised rifle barrel pointed at her from the stands. Gloria

Donner was squinting down the gun sight, only ten feet away. "Just because Wonder Boy messed up doesn't mean I will."

Nancy sucked in her breath. Gloria and Scott working together? Now everything made sense. It would have taken two people to plot out the scheme to get Colleen. One person—Gloria—who lived near Colleen, knew her every move and had access to the Healeys' barn. Gloria could have easily slipped the bouncing bet into Nightingale's stall. The other partner—Scott—was able to lurk out of sight at the show while Gloria pretended to be helpful. And both of them had had Colleen's trust.

"What is it that you want, Gloria?" Nancy called up to the trainer. Since the veil was still across Nancy's face, she hoped her voice would sound disguised.

"You don't know?" Gloria exclaimed incredulously. Then she laughed, a screeching sound that rang across the arena.

Oh, please let someone hear her! Nancy silently pleaded.

Abruptly the laughter stopped. "You're so naive, Colleen. That's what made it all so easy. I want *Nightingale*, of course. With Scott as her rider and me as her trainer, we'll go to the top. Not only will we make lots of money, but Scott will have his prize horse, and I'll have my reputation back."

"Wouldn't it be better to do it honestly? I could just sell her to you," Nancy fibbed nervously, hoping to stall Gloria.

The trainer snorted. "For what? Two hundred thousand? You think we have that kind of money?" She shook her head almost violently. "Nope. If my plan had worked, you would have been out of commission after your fall last night. I know your parents don't have the money for extra medical bills as well as a horse. With you unable to ride, Nightingale wouldn't be earning her keep. Posing as a friend of the family, I would have advised your parents to sell her while she's young and in top form. And, of course, since I'd be faithfully by your side at the hospital, your parents would have sold her to me—cheap!"

"So it was you who loosened that saddle," Nancy accused.

Gloria grinned. "Brilliant, huh? Too bad Nightingale's so smart. Any other horse would have taken off over that jump, and you would've flown fifteen feet in the air. There's no way you could have avoided getting injured."

"Maybe. But I don't understand," Nancy said, trying to get more information from Gloria. "Why did you poison the hay? And the nails in the stall, the yarn and the mask . . . ?"

"Theatrics," Gloria cut in. "Scott was the masked mystery man. All that stuff was to make sure the San Marcoses looked guilty. I didn't want those two getting hold of Nightingale if you

138

sold the horse. And the reason Scott locked you in the trailer was to make sure you'd be late for the Gambler's Choice, and too rattled to check your girth." She gave a low chuckle. "Much to our surprise, you made it through the first round without falling off. Luckily, I convinced you to ride in the jump-off."

"Sounds as if you thought of everything." Nancy looked back at Scott, who still hadn't moved. His horse was standing patiently across the ring, the reins dangling to the ground. "Aren't you going to get help for Scott?"

"Soon. But first I want to carry out plan number two." Gloria motioned toward Nightingale with the rifle barrel. "Get on. And if you think I won't shoot, guess again. I'm already in this deep, so there's no turning back."

Nancy froze. Gloria's crazy, she thought. If I don't do what she says, I'm dead.

"Get on!" Gloria screamed.

Quickly Nancy put her foot in the stirrup and mounted. "I don't get it," she said as she gathered the reins. "If you shoot me, the officials will realize it's not an accident."

"Ha! Don't you know anything?" Gloria reached up and patted the rifle. "This is a dart gun used to shoot tranquilizers. Only now it's loaded with a stimulant. One shot and Nightingale will be temporarily loco. She'll toss you sky high. Maybe this time you'll finally break your neck, and it'll look like an accident. By the time someone finds you, the stimulant will have worn off the horse. Then all I have to do is tell the officials that Scott, who was just trying to play a friendly Halloween prank on you, scared Nightingale. The mare panicked and you lost control.''

Gloria nodded to where Scott lay in the tanbark. "Actually, his fall makes a nice touch. Let's see. I can say he tried to save you and was thrown in the process.''

Nancy shook her head. "It'll never work. You'll never get Nightingale to hurt me.''

Gloria's grin disappeared. "Oh, yeah?" She waved the dart gun in the air. "If your horse doesn't, *I'll* figure out a way to finish you off. I'm sick of grooming for giggly debutantes who don't give a hoot about their horses. I want Nightingale. And I'll do anything to get her.''

"You won't get away with it. My friends and the security people will be here any second.''

Gloria raised her eyebrow. "Oh, really?" she said in mock surprise. "You mean that silly girl who was tied up and locked in the rest room is going to help? Or maybe you mean that boyfriend of yours, who we took care of. We made it look as though he fell in the stands and konked his head on the cement floor. Oh, yes, and then there's the ever-diligent security office. They didn't seem to mind at all when I called and canceled your little scheme.''

Nancy gasped. "How did you find out about that?''

140

Gloria snickered. "Lucky for me, I know the people who have horses next to Nightingale's stall. I helped groom their horse early this morning."

"You were eavesdropping on us?" Nancy was stunned.

"Like I said, brilliant, huh? Now ride."

As Nancy urged Nightingale into a trot, she racked her brains for a way out of the mess. But unless someone heard them in the arena, she was on her own.

She cast a fearful look over her shoulder. Gloria was walking away from the stands, moving toward the center of the arena—to get a better shot, Nancy figured. Maybe that means Gloria isn't an expert marksman, Nancy hoped. If I can just elude her until someone, anyone, gets here!

Tightening her reins, Nancy squeezed Nightingale into a canter. The mare responded quickly and smoothly. Out of the corner of her eye, Nancy spied Scott's black horse. His ears were pricked curiously as he watched Nightingale canter past.

With a tug on the left rein Nancy turned the mare toward the black horse. She remembered how Colleen had used Nightingale to round up the runaway in the warm-up ring. If she could just get Nightingale to go after the other horse! With both animals charging around the ring, Gloria would have a hard time hitting Nightingale.

141

"Yee-ha!" Waving one arm in the air, Nancy drove Nightingale toward the other horse. The black's head shot up and he spun on his back legs and took off.

Without any urging, Nightingale took off after him. Neck and neck, they raced down one side, then the other.

Nancy gripped Nightingale's mane and held on tight. She could hear Gloria screaming angrily. As long as they kept up this pace, Nancy reasoned, Gloria wouldn't be able to shoot Nightingale.

The question was—how long could the horses keep up this pace?

The two horses made a U-turn at the end of the arena and began to charge back, swerving around Scott's motionless body. The black horse was slowing, as if tired of the chase, and Nancy could feel Nightingale relaxing her pace.

Suddenly a loud whack made Nightingale jump. Nancy was thrown forward onto the mare's neck. Her legs flew behind her as she lost her balance.

"Whoa, girl." Nancy knew she had to slow Nightingale if she was going to stay on. Nightingale broke into a trot, and Nancy pushed herself back into the saddle. Quickly she glanced over her shoulder. A dart was sticking from the saddle panel. Nancy didn't think it had struck Nightingale.

"The next one's going to be it!" Gloria yelled.

She had vaulted into the arena and was heading toward them. In five more strides she would be close enough to shoot—and hit her mark.

Frantically Nancy looked around for a way to escape. Her best bet was to get off and run into the stands. But Gloria was so desperate, she'd probably shoot her with the gun. The drug might even kill her. But at least it would ruin Gloria's plan—an autopsy would show the drug in her body. The police would then have proof of foul play.

It's my only chance, Nancy thought. Her gaze rested on the exit gate. It was about five feet high, made of solid wood. Nightingale could probably jump it in her sleep.

Nancy's fingers tensed excitedly on the reins. At the same moment her heels dug into Nightingale's side. "Let's go, girl," she urged. "Show me what you can do!"

As she cantered toward the exit gate, Nightingale picked up speed. Her strides were sure and powerful. Nancy's insides were tied in a knot. This is crazy, she thought. But then she heard Gloria's voice screaming with frustration as she saw what Nancy was going to do.

"Here goes," Nancy said as Nightingale thundered closer to the gate. Suddenly Nancy was filled with horror. She'd underestimated the height of the gate. It was closer to seven feet high!

They'd never make it over.

16

Winners and Losers

It was too late to stop.

Nancy shut her eyes tightly and grabbed Nightingale's mane as the gate loomed in front of them. The mare took off. Tilting forward, Nancy rose in the stirrups. As if Nightingale had wings, she flew over the huge gate, landing with a jarring thud in the tanbark on the other side.

They'd made it!

Nancy came down hard in the saddle, lost both stirrups, and slipped sideways. Throwing her arms around Nightingale's neck, she hung on. The mare slowed to a trot. Ears pricked, she *clip-clopped* across the warm-up ring to the entrance of the stable area. Several early risers, grooming their horses, stared at them in surprise.

"Whoa, girl," Nancy was finally able to gasp. Nightingale halted and turned her head to gaze curiously at the person clinging to her neck.

Laughing with relief, Nancy slid to the ground. Her body felt wobbly, like rubber. Her fingers were stiff from clenching Nightingale's mane. Nancy's scarf and veil had flown off and were lying on the ground.

Marisa San Marcos came running over. "Nancy, are you all right? What's going on?"

Nancy shook her head. "I need to get security," she whispered urgently. Thrusting the reins into Marisa's hand, she stumbled, then ran up the stairs to the office.

She burst into the room and told the three startled officers to lock all the exit doors in the arena. To escape, Gloria would have to climb up to the main concourse. If they hurried, there was a chance they could catch her.

"And call an ambulance," Nancy added. "Someone's hurt in the ring." Motioning to one of the officers to follow, Nancy ran around the concourse and through the first door into the main arena.

Looking down at the ring, Nancy saw that Scott still hadn't moved. His horse was standing by the exit gate. Gloria was nowhere in sight.

Nancy's heart sank. She'd gotten away! But then Nancy saw movement across the arena. Gloria was bounding up the steps to the concourse, the rifle still in her hand.

"There she goes!" Nancy cried. One of the officers switched on his radio mike and called for reinforcements. But Nancy wasn't going to take any chances. Quickly she decided it would be faster to go across the arena than all the way around the concourse.

Nancy leapt down the steps to the arena below. Gloria was about halfway to the door when Nancy saw someone suddenly hurtle from behind a row of seats and tackle the trainer. The rifle flew into the air. Gloria and her pursuer crashed to the floor and began to roll down the steps. Nancy recognized Phil's dark hair and blue shirt.

Leaping over the arena wall, Nancy sprinted across the ring. The security officer was right behind her. Nancy couldn't see Phil and Gloria. They'd rolled to the bottom row of seats, disappearing from view behind the wall.

In record time Nancy reached the other side. Breathless, she grabbed the top of the wall and pulled herself up. Below her she could see Phil fighting with Gloria. He had her pinned, but the stocky woman was clawing like a wildcat. Nancy climbed over the wall and jumped to the floor.

"You'll never take me in!" Gloria screamed. Then she caught sight of Nancy. For a moment she stopped struggling as she realized that the person in the Arabian costume hadn't been Colleen. Then her face screwed up into a horrible grimace.

"You tricked me!" she screeched. "Pretending you were Colleen! Nightingale would have been mine if you hadn't meddled." With a roar of anger Gloria rose up, tossing Phil aside as if he wasn't even there. Then she threw herself at Nancy's legs.

146

Propelled backward, Nancy crashed into the seat behind her. Suddenly Gloria's angry face was looming over her, grinning wickedly. Quickly Nancy drew her knee back and kicked Gloria in the stomach.

"Oof." The stocky woman grunted, doubling over. Phil and the security officer each grabbed one of her arms and twisted them behind her. Then the security officer snapped on handcuffs.

By this time the second officer had made it down the steps. The two officers and Phil pulled Gloria away from Nancy. The woman put up a struggle for a moment, then gave up. She glared maliciously at Nancy as she was dragged away.

"I hope you called the police," the first officer said to his partner. "This one needs to cool off in jail." The other man nodded as they started up the stairs with Gloria.

"She's got to be nuts." Phil shook his head as he watched her being led away. Then he reached down and pulled Nancy to her feet. "Are you okay? That was a rough fall."

Nancy rubbed her shoulder where she'd landed. She was worried about Bess but wanted to make sure Phil was all right, too. "I'm all in one piece," Nancy said. "How about you? Gloria told me she'd put you out of commission."

"And how." Phil lowered his head, grimacing when Nancy touched the back of it. His hair was sticky with blood.

"Looks like a nasty blow. When the medics get

147

here for Scott, you'd better have them examine it."

"So the Headless Horseman was Scott," Phil said in disbelief.

"Mmm." Breathing deeply, Nancy looked over at the still body. "Believe me, I was just as surprised as you were."

"I wondered who it was. I saw him ride through the gate, then wham! Gloria must have hit me with the rifle butt, and I blacked out." Phil gingerly touched his head. "I started coming to just as Gloria was about to shoot you."

Suddenly Phil grinned. "By the way, nice jump. That gate's about seven feet tall. A little higher and you would have broken the world's indoor high-jump record."

Nancy laughed. "Believe me, it wasn't by choice. But now I know why people say Nightingale's such a wonder horse."

Just then the rescue squad roared into the ring. "Security must have gotten the gate unlocked," Nancy said, starting up the steps. "I'm going to find Bess, then check on Nightingale. That horse is in good hands, though. Marisa has her. By now she's probably fed Nightingale a hundred carrots and spoiled her with brushing."

Phil chuckled. "I'll head down to the rescue truck. I want to call Colleen as soon as I can, too. She'll be worried sick."

Nancy broke into a jog as soon as she reached the concourse. It was six A.M., and a few yawning vendors were setting up for the day.

Gloria had said that Bess was tied up in one of the rest rooms. The trainer must have intercepted her somewhere on the way to the security office.

Nancy backtracked to the steps that Bess would have taken from the warm-up ring. Then she took the same path down the concourse. Nancy spied a men's room and finally the ladies' room. In between the two rooms was a horse trailer display. Gloria could have hidden behind the trailer and jumped Bess when she walked past.

The rest room door was unlocked, but the light was off. Nancy flicked it on. "Bess?" she called.

A frantic "Ho ur ere!" came from the far stall. Nancy ran back and swung open the door. Bess was wedged between the wall and the toilet. Her mouth was taped and her hands and feet had been trussed together with leg wraps, just like Colleen's had been.

"Bess! Are you all right?" Nancy knelt on the cold floor and began to peel the tape off her mouth.

"No!" Bess sputtered. "I'm freezing cold. Get me out of here!"

Nancy grinned. Her friend appeared to be fine. When Nancy had unwound the wraps, Bess immediately jumped up.

"So tell me what happened," she said as the two of them left the rest room. "I hope you caught Gloria. I couldn't believe it when I saw it was her. She jumped me from behind—threw me right on the floor. Before I knew it, she had

149

that tape over my mouth. Then she twisted my arms behind my back and pushed me into the bathroom." Bess rubbed her wrists. "Wow, was she strong!"

Nancy nodded. "Yeah. We got her, though. And Scott, too."

"Scott!" Bess's eyes flew wide with surprise. "But how, when . . ." she stammered.

Nancy put a finger to her lips. "Let's go get Nightingale, and I'll tell you all about it."

That night Phil, Bess, and Nancy were sitting in the stands, watching Nightingale and Colleen finish a perfect round in the Worthington Cup. When the duo trotted from the ring, the audience clapped and whistled.

"Whew." Nancy let out her breath. "I can't believe how well everything ended. Just this morning Nightingale was dodging Gloria's darts."

"At least she dodged them." Phil chuckled. He had a bandage on the back of his head. "Luckily, that's the last we'll see of Gloria and Scott. The officials barred them from ever participating in any show recognized by the American Horse Show Association. That means their careers are over for good."

"As well as their big dream to go all the way to the top." Nancy shook her head. "It's too bad they were in such a hurry. They were both talented enough to be winners on their own. And now Gloria's in jail, and Scott's in the hospital with his hip in a cast."

"I think they both lost sight of reality," Phil said. "Scott was too obsessed with getting revenge, and Gloria was driven by ambition. Together they must have thought they were invincible."

"And they almost were!" Bess put in.

"The Capital Center is pressing charges," Phil continued. "But still, Gloria and Scott will probably just be fined and put on probation. Gloria's already made up some story about how she didn't know the gun was loaded with a stimulant. She told the police she thought she had tranquilizer darts to use on Scott's horse after the horse went crazy and threw him off. She claims that's what made Nightingale spook."

"Wow. Gloria really had it all planned out," Bess said. "She's crazy, all right."

"That's for sure," Nancy agreed. "And after all, it's our word against theirs. Who's going to believe I was chased by a Headless Horseman?"

They all laughed. Then Marisa trotted into the ring on Mr. Sunshine. The buzzer sounded, and the young girl on her flashy bay circled smoothly and headed for the first jump.

"I'm really glad Colleen's seriously talking to the San Marcoses about Nightingale," Phil said. "I think Marisa's one of the best riders around. She's kind, enthusiastic, and talented."

"What about Diego?" Bess grumbled. "He's such a big grump."

Nancy laughed at her friend's sour expression. "Give the guy a chance, Bess. I spent this afternoon with Diego while Marisa and Colleen were talking. He's really a nice guy—just a little old-fashioned and strict. Marisa's got the guts and ability. He's got the discipline."

Bess shrugged. "I guess. Hey, did you see that jump?" Mr. Sunshine turned the corner and galloped to the last obstacle, a high wall. He leapt, touching the top brick with his front hoof. It fell to the ground.

"That's four faults," Phil explained. "Colleen's still ahead."

"Let's go on down to the warm-up ring," Nancy said, standing. "I want to congratulate both of them on their rounds."

When they reached the crowded ring, Colleen was astride Nightingale, talking to Diego. Marisa had dismounted and was standing next to them, holding Mr. Sunshine. Nancy noticed that Marisa had a huge smile on her face.

"What's going on?" Nancy asked when she reached them.

"She's mine!" Marisa flung her arms around Nightingale's neck.

"Not exactly," Diego told his daughter in a patient voice. "She's yours to ride and show, yes. But not yours to keep."

"Mine, mine, mine," Marisa chanted as if she didn't hear her father.

Everyone laughed.

"So what's the deal?" Phil asked, looking up at Colleen with a big smile. Nancy knew that the news had made him very pleased. She just hoped Colleen was happy, too.

With a sigh her friend dismounted. "Diego made me an offer I couldn't refuse," Colleen said. Nancy noticed a tear in her friend's eye, but then Colleen broke into a smile. "I'm going to lease Nightingale to him and Marisa, starting in January. That way she'll still be mine, Marisa will get to show her, and I'll have enough money to go to college!"

"And the best thing," Marisa added, her face beaming, "is that when we retire Nightingale and Colleen gets her back, we're going to get her first foal!"

"What finally made you come to a decision?" Phil asked Colleen. "Nightingale's done so well at the show. I figured you'd be ready to take her to Florida for the winter circuit."

"She was superb," Colleen said. "Which proved to me that Nightingale should be with someone who will take her to the top." She nodded toward Marisa. "I just don't have the interest and the drive anymore. Besides, it was so hard finding out about Scott and Gloria. . . ." She shook her head sadly. "I mean, I thought they were my friends. How could I have been so blind?"

"Hey, we were all fooled," Nancy said.

"I know, but that doesn't help much," Colleen said. "Seeing how obsessed they were made me put winning horse shows in perspective. I want to do something more in my life, and now I can—without having to give up Nightingale."

"Wow." Bess sniffed. "This is like the ending of a great movie."

"One with lots of action." Phil chuckled. "I wish you guys could have seen Nancy and Nightingale jumping that gate."

"Don't remind me," Nancy groaned. "I'll be having nightmares forever."

Just then a voice over the loudspeaker announced, "First place and the Worthington Cup Trophy goes to Ms. Colleen Healey and Nightingale!"

For a moment Colleen looked startled, as if she didn't believe it.

"Go on!" Marisa urged. "Jog in there on Nightingale and get the trophy!"

"Oh, right!" Colleen said finally. Then she turned and threw her arms around Nancy. "But there's someone who deserves that trophy more than me. My friend, Nancy Drew, the best detective around!"